WHAT IF ROALD DAHL WROTE ALL ABOUT... 2022
Copyright © 2022 by Geoff Bunn & Cheryl Harding

First Printing: 2022
**ISBN:** 9798359297493

# What if

# ROALD DAHL

# wrote ALL ABOUT...

# 2022

GEOFF BUNN

&

CHERYL HARDING

# Contents

# Introduction

We invent borders so that we can invent countries. Then we invent national flags, and we invent nationalist songs (a.k.a. anthems), to celebrate those invented lands of ours. Then we invent armies, and we invent weapons to give to those armies, to fight for those invented countries. And then we are horrified at the results of war.

We invent money so that we can invent prices for essential items such as food, housing and healthcare. We invent an elite, at the top of society, to whom we give most of that money. Then we invent punishments for those at the bottom, who can no longer afford the bare essentials of life.

We invent machines, which run on limited natural resources, to drive us to invented jobs, where we produce innumerable invented consumer goods that most of us, really, have only an invented need for. Then we wonder what to do with all the waste, pollution and inequality we have created by producing those same consumer goods.

When will we, as a species, ever learn? If we can invent all of those things — things which, had we not invented them, would otherwise not exist — then why-oh-why can't we invent ways of living in peace and of sharing and of caring for one another and this precious world of ours? Of working *with* the planet rather than against it?

Welcome to 2022. Another year where the only 'intelligent' species on the planet makes an almost total mess of absolutely everything!

*I'd like to take this opportunity to say a big & special thankyou to Cheryl Harding, for her contributions to this book. Fingers crossed that we will NOT need to write another one of these in 2023...*

# The OMG strain

"Omega. Really? Gosh. Omega. That sounds very like OMG, doesn't it?" The Prime Minister chuckled.

The First Advisor, a thin man with even thinner spectacles, glanced at the Second Advisor. The Second Advisor, a large woman with an even larger hairdo, gave a small but hardly perceptible shrug. Meetings were never easy these days. Not with 'him' in charge.

"Truly, I had not particularly noticed any such similarity", said the First Advisor, advisedly. After all, being advised with words was one of the many talents required to succeed in such a position. The clue to that being in the job title: advisor.

"OMG. Omega. OMG. Omega. Hee, hee".

"Yes, Prime Minister", said the First Advisor. "Quite. I suppose there is a certain humour to be found within the name".

"I mean, if you say it out loud. You know, if you actually pronounce the OMG letters, oh, emm, gee. It is identical, isn't it?"

It wasn't identical. But it tickled the big pink PM anyway. And he did enjoy being tickled by things. Especially silly things.

"And when you think about it, to be honest, you have to wonder why they didn't name all the dratted variants like that, eh?" guffawed the Prime Minister. "Or, at least, you know, gave them all similarly funny names".

Somebody in the room sighed. Very, very heavily.

Faces turned. Looked from one to another.

Who was it? Who had sighed?

Nobody owned up.

It could have been anyone.

Or perhaps it was the room itself which sighed. After all, the cabinet meeting room had seen it all. Great moments in history, great leaders. Men and women, like them or not, such as Disraeli, Gladstone, Churchill, Attlee, Wilson, Thatcher... yet somehow, in recent years, the oak panelling could just as easily have been replaced with straw bales and a large canvas tent. Government had become a circus. And a circus led by a clown.

"Yes. Well, anyway, the thing is erm...", continued the First Advisor, reedy voice desperately wanting to get this meeting over with so that he, and his colleagues, could get out of the madhouse and return to their real jobs of actually trying to run the country. "Well. We've now received the detailed briefing on this variant of the virus from our counterparts in Brazil".

Brazil. Oh dear.

Now that was an unfortunate choice of word.

The Home Secretary cleared her throat at the mention of that country. It was somewhere foreign. And she didn't like Brazilians. Not one bit. To her, they were a dark and distant sort who ought to have cut down that big forest of theirs, rather than keep complaining about it, and sold the wood off log by log. (Which, in practice, was actually happening. But that made no difference to how she felt about them).

But then... to be fair... the Home Secretary didn't like anybody. It wasn't just South Americans. She didn't like any non-Europeans. Nor even most Europeans. Nor the Scottish, nor the Irish nor the Welsh. Nor, really, did she like anyone from north of Watford. Nor did she care a great deal for very many of those from south of Watford either. She even argued, regularly, with her own reflection.

Hearing that clearing, however, the Second Advisor quickly sprang to the rescue. "It's erm... er... it's all researchers and scientists. All Oxbridge trained. You know. They just happen to be working in Brazil at the moment. On our behalf".

"Ah!" said the Home Secretary. "Well then, that's more like it".

"OMG", said the Prime Minister, a tad quieter now, but still chuckling at the word. "Omega. OMG. I mean, why call it the Indian or Ceylon variant, that only makes it sound like a tea? I've got the Ceylon variant. Oh, really, do you drink that with lemon or milk? Hee, hee. One lump or two?"

"And what do *they* say?" said the Home Secretary. "Our experts". Trying to turn the meeting back to the reports from Brazil.

"Well...", began the First Advisor, evidently the news was going to be bad. "Well... it is, actually, quite a surprise".

The room waited.

Breaths were baited.

The First Advisor was more than used to breaking bad news to the people seated around this table. After all, they seemed to lurch from one near-disaster to another these days. But this new chunk of bad news was different. Very different. Because the news from Brazil itself was actually rather good. It wasn't bad at all.

The trouble was, the government had not waited to hear the news before hitting the 'Big Red National Panic Button', and in recent weeks the whole gamut of panicky laws and restrictions had duly been brought back into force: shops had closed, masks once more made compulsory, testing ramped up, football and other sporting events cancelled (though not the horse racing, of course, as that would be going too far), theatres and museums closed (but then, who cared about those things anyway?), schoolchildren were once more dressed up in masks on a Monday, then sent home on a

Tuesday because, during assembly, somebody coughed, a little tiny cough, and parents were being driven slowly but surely insane with the endless chopping and changing... basically, everything. The whole lot. Everything. All over again. International trade had been wound down. Housing problems ramped up. Furloughs increased, debt increased, stress increased. Newspaper headlines had all-too-willingly screamed 'Omega Terror - Everyone urged to stay indoors for at least THREE MONTHS and not breathe more than absolutely necessary' and, to cap it all, the usual suspects on TV had sent miserable-faced journalists all over the world to find images of thin donkeys or bemused Algerian bar staff in order to illustrate quite what a devastating effect the Omega variant was having on everyone, everywhere.

And it was. Actually. The new variant of the virus *was* having a devastating effect. It was having a devastating effect *because* of all those measure which had been taken.

But the variant itself?

The new strain of doom?

The end of humanity as we all knew it?

The First Advisor had no idea how to tell the truth of the matter to this Prime Minister, nor indeed to any of the other good folk who sat around the table either asleep and snoring or folding paper planes or, in one peculiar instance, doing both.

"OMG", said the Prime Minister again, though a bit quieter now. "I must put that one on Twitter. Should score a few brownie points, eh? Pickaninny points, you might say. Hee, hee. No offence, Home Secretary".

"None taken", snapped the Home Secretary, who actually, generally, took offence at everything and everyone.

"Go on", whispered the Second Advisor. "Tell them all, for goodness sake. So we can get out of here".

The First Advisor sighed. There was nothing for it. Spit it out. The only way to go. "Well, it's erm... it's actually not... I mean the Omega variant itself isn't... erm... it seems it isn't actually all that dangerous."

"Not really. Not actually very much", added the Second Advisor. "Well, not at all in fact. More just like a cold, really. A common cold. Old and fragile people can be susceptible... especially the poorer ones, but the rest of us? No. Not really".

"OMG", said the PM.

"Oh do shut up!" snapped the Home Secretary

And with that silence briefly reigned in the room.

A very loud silence.

"Please, go on", said the Home Secretary. "About the report, I mean".

"Well", said the First Advisor. "In fact, they conclude that it might be the best possible thing if we simply allow this one, this variant, to spread. And quickly, too. As, with it generally being so mild, it will give everyone a natural immunity. Which, I think we all now realise, is the only sustainable way forwards. Out of this pandemic, so to speak...".

His voice tailed off.

The Prime Minister wasn't listening. Not really. Having been told to shut-up, he was now deep in admiration of his new tie. Which was blue and silver and flecked with gold. Though, admittedly, the gold bits were actually stains from his boiled eggs that morning.

"Eggs", he muttered. "Never been able to eat one of the tricky things, without getting it all over the old tie".

A heavy clock on the mantelpiece ticked. Then it tocked. As clocks are inclined to do. Following, logically, every tick with a tock.

"Nanny used to say that gravy was the worst, though", said the PM, looking up at all the losing-patience faces which surrounded the table. "An egg, it almost dips itself in one's tie. But gravy, different thing altogether. It splish-splashes all over the shop, what? Never wear a white shirt when scoffing a nose-bag full of mash and gravy. That's what I always say". He stopped rambling. Looked back down at the tie. Looked up again at the incredibly angry expression now being worn by his Home Secretary. "What, what?" he said. "So, it's all good news then, about the OMG variant, what? Back to normal we all go? Jolly good. Jolly good. Shall we have a party to celebrate, then? I still have a few bottles of champers left over... in a drawer somewhere or other... from one of our parties, you know."

It was true that this particular Home Secretary always had an angry expression. Often, in fact, bordering on the furiously livid. Whether that was down to a personality issue of some kind (which, actually, it was), or whether she just had one of those bulldog-chewing-a-wasp faces, it was hard to say. Either way around, on this occasion, and not withstanding the Prime Minister's endless and hopelessly inane banter, she was very, very, very livid, again.

"Whhaaaaattt?" she fumed. "Never mind the ramblings of this oaf, just you run that by me once more, young man!"

The First Advisor, not young, but quite definitely a man, shuddered. Hoping, briefly, that it was not to him the Home Secretary was referring. But it was. "I'm sorry?" he said.

"That!" said the Home Secretary, standing, then sitting, glowering, standing again and pointing a long and unpleasantly hooked finger in the direction of the report, from which the Advisors had both been reading.

"Ah, yes", said the First Advisor. "I know, yes. It is erm... politically... yes, it is erm... But then, to be fair, every nation in the world, barring Sweden, has done the very same thing. Same things. We've all made the same piggies ear out of this latest variant. Panicked, a tad. A lot, in fact. All governments have done it. So its not just us".

The Second Advisor stepped in to help. "And it *is* very good news, really", she suggested tentatively.

"It is?" said the Home Secretary, glowering at everyone and everything, everywhere, all at one and the same moment.

The Second Advisor realised she ought not have spoke. But it was too late now. That had been a no going back sort of moment. "Well it could mean the end of the virus", said the Second Advisor, her tone rather sheepish. "And as the PM suggests, back to normality and all that. Soonish, anyway".

"That is certainly a possibility", agreed the First Advisor. "In the very near future".

"No more locking people in, I mean 'lockdowns', no more restrictions on travel or trade....".

"No more deaths. The NHS getting back to normal".

"No more banging saucepans".

The words were uttered. They were meant to help. In the sea of positivity and optimism which would flow from the end, or potential end, of the virus, the political damage of the hastily organised national Omega shutdown would surely be forgotten. Pandemic Over: this was the news everyone had waited to hear. For two years. An end to the headlines and divisions and costs and stresses and deaths.

But no.

Clearly the Home Secretary was not impressed.

Far from it, in fact.

"Back to normal?" she growled. "Are you mad? Normal? Do you have any idea, I mean ANY idea, just how much money some of our friends have been making these last two years from masks and tests and selling equipment and dysfunctional IT systems and the like?"

"Ah, that, yes", said the Second Advisor. "Yes. Yes, there is that. Yes. Some folk have done very nicely out of those things, that much is true".

"And", continued the Home Secretary, who was never the sort of woman one could interrupt. "And do you have any idea as to how much MORE could have been made, which we all now we stand to lose if the news about this blasted new variant gets out, and if the damn thing puts an end to the pandemic? For goodness sake, we'd need a major war in Europe or something to start making anything like the same levels of profits!"

War. Europe. Surely not? But then... politics was always a dirty old game.

"Well, no. I don't have the *exact* figures, no", said the Second Advisor. "Though I am sure we could get those for you if you need them. I believe we hired a firm of consultants only last week who could calculate...".

The Prime Minister suddenly chuckled. Loudly. "Omega. OMG. The OMG variant". He turned to look at the Foreign Secretary. "They grow tea now, in Yorkshire, apparently. Did you know that? I never knew. Tea. But isn't that a wonderful thing? British innovation, I suppose. World leading. World leading".

# A better world?

The realisation had made all the difference.

Doctor Rooker knew that. He knew the whole story very well.

After all, he had trained as a doctor for seven years, and then, in order to specialise in this particular field, he had undergone two further years of training. And a part of that, an important part of that, those extra two years, was understanding the history behind the subject, and the reason for the surgery now being so widespread.

Admittedly, his training was, by now, a good few years back in his past. His own past. He had done all of that stuff, the learning, way back in his twenties. And now, a few months short of fifty, more often than not, he found his mind wandering away from psychology and surgery, and onto the topic of an early and comfortable retirement.

But such was life.

That was how things were now.

Things had changed a lot in the last century or so. And it would be wonderful, quite, quite wonderful, to finish work and get out into the world and enjoy life.

Because retirement was now at fifty.

For everyone.

And hadn't that been a major part of his own reasoning for going into this whole field?

Yes. Yes it had been.

Prior to the realisation, retirement ages were continually being pushed back. The state, so states had claimed back then, could no longer afford to pay people a pension.

That was what they used to say. Back then.

But so much else, *back then*, had been a chaotic mish-mash of lies and incompetence too.

The way the world had been going at that time? Well... it had not been good. Not good at all. His own father had only been a child of five at the time the Netherlands was largely washed out to sea. Global warming being to blame for that.

And now? He smiled. Almost laughed. Today people in Europe barely recollected things like bananas and pineapples. They still appeared, rarely, from time to time, in the most up-market of shops. But even then, that was only for special occasions. And long gone were the days where exotic stuff like that filled the shelves of every corner super-market.

It was unsustainable.

It had always been unsustainable.

Then the climate had snapped. Changed. Broken. Whatever you wanted to call it. And it had done so because of humanity. Of that there was no doubt.

In order to make a fast buck, for a few, and to have some home comforts — the majority of which we didn't really need — we had almost, not quite but almost, totally ruined our own planet.

And then the realisation had... happened.

And the world had changed. Quickly. So, so quickly. Not exactly overnight, because that simply wasn't possible. But quickly all the same.

And in the space of one single century all the pressure had gone. The world had breathed an enormous sigh of relief.

Because the trouble with the world, back then, in a nutshell, had been overpopulation. As simple as that.

Sure, we used up our limited fossil fuels, poisoned our rivers and farmlands with chemicals, we wasted our efforts on manufacturing plastic nonsense, continually changing fashions, all sorts of things, you name it. But, fundamentally, it was, actually, all quite sustainable so long as there were less of us.

A lot less of us.

Like... half as many. To begin with.

And then, even less.

A lot less.

Of course most of that was before Doctor Rooker's time.

Just like that pandemic. Way back, one hundred years ago. The year 2020, or thereabouts. Covid. The world had missed a chance there to reduce its human population. When the Covid virus first appeared it killed, and it killed the old. And it should, so the history books all now agreed, have been allowed to run riot. Why? Because it could have reduced the global population by a quarter. Maybe more. Who knew how much? Just like the Black Death had once done.

But no, that opportunity had been missed.

Vaccines had seen to that.

And that virus had mellowed over time.

An opportunity missed.

Then things, over the next few decades or so, into the 2030s, 2040s and 2050s had become impossible.

Crops were failing on a prodigious scale, wars, other diseases, mass migration, drought. You name it. All doubled, tripled, quadrupled in scale.

That had been a horrible time. Apparently.

The worst period in human history.

Or so the history books said.

Personally, Doctor Rooker did not believe, had never believed, that Covid would have helped with any of that. At least, not very much. Even by 2020, humanity was already too far gone, as a species. It had left things to fall apart for too long.

He yawned. A huge yawn.

And then turned to look, for a while, out of his office window.

The world today? Wow. What a difference. It looked a much happier, healthier place. It really did.

People had space now.

And resources enough to go around.

No. No. Be more accurate than that. Resources were now plentiful. Plentiful. That was the truth of it. Shortages were a thing of the past. Of the bad old days. Now, whatever people wanted, they could have. It was as simple as that.

And the reason for that? Mass depopulation.

It had worked.

Just as if a Black Death or whatever had struck.

But this had been no disease.

No accident.

No great tragedy.

This had been deliberate. Paced, steady, but deliberate.

And, more importantly, the global population was still, slowly, declining. Even more than it had already declined.

All of which was terrific news.

Doctor Rooker checked his watch. One more appointment today, then home time. Back to his house, tennis court and pool. Only a stones throw away. A short but pleasant walk. Under a clear blue sky, no longer filled with contrails from aircraft.

Was it clear and blue today? He half-ducked his head to see out of the window. To look up at the sky.

Yes. Clear. And blue. The light as crystal as it must have been long before the first human ever walked the earth.

Doctor Rooker laughed at that idea. Well, perhaps that was a bit of an exaggeration. But certainly, these days, the sky was a lot clearer than it had been for hundreds of years.

Clear? Yes. And clean too! The air had been toxic once. Before he was born. And even, if he recollected it correctly, for a few years after he was born. That was true. And it was the realisation that had changed it all.

He checked his watch again.

There was time enough to finish the crossword in the newspaper. Surely? Yes. Yes, there was.

The Doctor picked up his pen. And, for a few moments, frowned at the puzzle. There were a few clues, today, which he simply could not resolve.

He tried.

But no.

Ah well. No matter. He would ask Elke about it, back at home. She was great at crosswords. And she would be there later. She had pencilled him in — or should that be penned in — for a few hours together. And he was looking forward to seeing her again.

Doctor Rooker put his newspaper down. And looked, once more, out of the window at the wide, clear, clean streets beyond.

He smiled. A broad smile.

Why such a big smile? Because a man, across the road, was busy watching something or other up the street whilst his dog, possibly knowing that his owners attention was elsewhere, peed over his trouser leg.

Eventually the man, presumably feeling a little damp on his leg, looked down at the dog. And spoke to the animal.

Not angrily.

No. Not angrily.

Anger was a rarity these days. Almost unheard of.

The Doctor looked back at his watch.

It was funny really, just like that man outside with his dog, the whole world had been 'looking the wrong way' for a solution to its problems. Back then. Looking the wrong way and finding no answers. Things had just gone on getting worse, in fact.

For a start, people had been talking for ages about 'How to make cities sustainable'. Well, the answer to that question was simple: cities were not, and never could be, sustainable.

All kinds of effort, technological, environmental, financial, you name it, had been poured into cities. Trying to make them 'work'. But they did not work, and would never work.

Cities were unnatural. And they had to go.

Then there were schools. Children. Kids. The whole family thing.

Pretty much every single problem in the world came back to that one single issue: children.

Because a family that had kids, wanted and felt they needed possessions. Property. Savings. Inheritance. Stuff to pass on to the youngsters. A cosy home. Summer holidays. Christmas presents. School uniforms, school books.

Goodness me, you name it. And the amount of money that was spent on schools, not to mention paediatric care, in one form or another.

It was insane.

Likewise the world, back then, spent a fortune, an absolute fortune, on healthcare for kids. And, in turn, it had to be said, on healthcare for women too.

Schools, cities, apartments, healthcare, you name it.

So much of that was aimed at, intended for, directed towards women and towards children. The family.

And it was unaffordable.

Off the scale.

That was the truth of it.

The global population was completely out of control, and yet we were pouring money into children. In one form or another.

Madness.

Doctor Rooker laughed. Yes. Back then, just as with the man outside with the dog, the world was looking the wrong way.

The realisation had made all the difference.

Women, not men, were the problem.

Women.


Men were fine. Left alone, without kids, without all those ties to families and what have you, without the need to provide, without the need or desire to pass on any inheritance... men were fine. No need to be aggressive, no need to work tirelessly, no sexism, no possessions. No more central heating. No more inheritance. No more jealousies. No more need for male to show off.

It was all of *that stuff* which had been dragging the world down.

Men did not need women. Nor did they need children.

And had it not been for that realisation, the world would have gone on in the same old way, and the whole planet would have burned.

Sex?

Companionship?

That was easy.

That was what men like Doctor Rooker took care of.

His final appointment of the day, would be a gender re-assignment. Or, at least, a primary consultation for a full reassignment. Some ops were partial and some ops were full. It all depended. The choice was entirely down to the individual. Either way around, trans-women had replaced females. Men found such women to be sexier, more fun, less demanding and, of course, it meant no children and no family. And with that... all of that... gone were all of those other problems, too.

The world was now a much, much, better, cleaner, safer and healthier place.

Doctor Rooker shook his head. No wonder some women had been so opposed to trans women. How on earth had it taken so long to realise where the real problem lay?

# Just an old tin pot

The old tin pot wanted war.

Or, at least, a great big battle.

A splurge. A fight. A punch-up.

Something.

Just anything.

The last surviving aluminium saucepan from a once handsome set which had been produced in the 1950s, the pot brooded endlessly on the subject of life, whilst sitting on the very top shelf of the pantry.

But wait!

Stop!

What exactly *is* a pantry? If you're under the age of fifty or so, you might have no idea.

And why was the tin pot sitting in a pantry and brooding on the subject of life?

Well... one thing at a time.

Rare these days, a pantry was a once familiar feature in most homes. A sort of walk-in, kitchen cupboard.

And very useful they were, too.

Long before fridges and freezers were invented, long before microwaves, food processors, ready meals, widespread obesity, mass food waste and irritable bowels, the pantry was the place where we stored all our food. Butter and milk, cheese and bread, carrots, yesterday's turkey and tins of ham or jars of pickle would all be kept on it's deep and dark and cool shelves with nothing but dust, calmness and the odd spider for company.

*That* was a pantry.

Of course, it goes without saying that the vast majority of homes today no longer have such cool and functional spaces. This is partly because they (modern homes) are far too small to have one, and partly because people today are no longer supposed to cook. You should now to go to work, come home, stuff in something indigestible, listen to the gloomiest of news programs, go to bed, sleep badly and then start all over again the following morning.

But out in the sticks... in comfy homes where people have plenty of money, lots of time off and much less stress... things out there are quite different. And pantries can still be found in big old houses of the sort that never change hands and never have roads or industrial units or housing estates built within sight or earshot.

And the pantry in this particular story is situated in one of those great big homes.

And it was on the top shelf of this particular pantry, that the old tin pot sat and brooded about life.

Ah, but now, next question, why was it brooding?

In fact it takes a little bit of imagination to understand why a big, old aluminium saucepan should ever feel the need to brood. Never mind turn it's attentions to the problems of life.

So I'll explain.

In the first place, the pan (or pot) had been made in the 1950s, which is a long time ago, and so it now felt rather old and tired. And as any old and tired person will tell you, there are days when you feel fed-up and cannot really manage to do very much else other than brood.

But there was also more to it than that. Just consider the life of a saucepan for a moment...

The world is tough for pots and pans. Time passes, you wait on a shelf or in a cupboard, then someone reaches for you, hauls you down, fills you up with a liquid, sometimes freezing cold but sometimes already boiling hot. Then, without so much as a by-your-leave, your are stuffed full with potatoes or carrots, with meat or sauce or stew or soup. And then your bottom is stuck on top of a naked flame and you are generally heated up a fair old whack.

And it doesn't stop there!

Once you have been boiled, or mashed, or bashed, or emptied, you then have a forced soak in a bath of hot water and soap suds, where a very rough cloth called a dishcloth is used to scour your insides spotlessly clean.

So, overall, being a saucepan is not a lifestyle to envy.

But pots and pans are made of sterner stuff than us, which is why they do the cooking and we do the eating. And, if you asked one, it would probably tell you that it much preferred to be so brusquely used, rather than stuck to one side or left on a dark, dusty shelf, and quite forgotten about. Never to be used any more.

And that would probably apply in triplicate, if not quintuplicate, to a big old 1950s aluminium saucepan that had once been the focal point of the Sunday dinner or midweek soup.

Gone were the days that your lid was removed to 'oohs' and 'aaahs', smiling family faces and the grey-soapy smell of overcooked cabbage.

Gone were the times you sat with pride of place on the kitchen table, being slowly served from, watching those around you fill themselves up with your hidden delights.

Gone was cooking.

Gone was Bisto.

Gone were home deliveries of dark brown beer and gone were graded grains which made finer flour.

Times change. Things move on. Some for the better, some not.

And now, all there was left to do, even in a big old wealthy house like this one out in Shireshire, was to sit, forlorn and forgotten, on a top shelf, in the big old pantry, and wonder whatever happened to it all.

And *that* was why this particular tin pot sat brooding.

In short, it was proper, well and truly, fed up.


"Bah", said the old tin pot, "I deserve better than this!"

It peered over the edge of the shelf upon which it say, trying hard to see some, any, of the various other forgotten or broken items and utensils with which it now shared it's fading existence in the shadowlands of the pantry.

But in the gloom of that darkened space, it wasn't at all easy to see anything.

Perhaps there, the edge of a potato slicer? A thing from the Sixties. Useless. Parts of which were even plastic. Plastic of all things! Grrr.

And perhaps there, just along the shelf, to the left a little, there was a nice red saucepan lid? Metal. A proper lid for a proper saucepan, of the same colour and type which had once belonged to the big tin pot. But much smaller. For the pot had lost it's own red lid many years earlier.

"How dare you all ignore me! I deserve BETTER THAN THIS!" it shouted. "I was the biggest pot in this house once! And the most important!"

Once. Yes. Back in the day.

But not any more.

How to deal with being ignored now?

How best to deal with being forgotten about today?

Sitting here, on the shelf, slowly but remorselessly ageing, would only lead to one thing: a quick trip, sooner or later, to the recycling bin. There to be melted down and turned into parts for a lightweight bicycle. Spending the rest of time being carried up and down the Peak District on busy bank-holidays weekends by some earnest type who worked during the week as a private doctor specialising expensively in haemorrhoids.

No, no! That would not do!

But how, how, how to get attention?

What did people do, these days, if they wanted to be seen or heard?

The tin pot sat back a little.

Thinking. (Or, if you prefer, brooding).

"Perhaps I should make a Tik Tok video?" it said to itself.

But no. Of course not. That was hardly the way forward for an old saucepan. Once the pride of the aluminium revolution. Nor was it really all that practicable for a pot to make a video. Even holding the phone, to film oneself, would prove extraordinarily difficult. Besides, the pan wasn't young and it wasn't pretty, so who would watch it's Tik Tok?

"Or perhaps I should spend a few months on a desert island, surrounded by scantily clad young men and women, cameras watching my every move?"

But no. Of course not. That may have been a great idea for a lissom twenty something or an MP with no sense of duty, but a saucepan? Even were it accepted onto the desert island - it would surely be the first thing rejected from the set and sent back home. Back home yes, quite possibly, and maybe not even allowed back into the pantry!

So no. No, no, no.

The days where one could become famous for splitting an atom or cracking a genetic code like... like er... like whassername... like those people had... were long over.

Now it was all instant this, immediate the other. And saucepans were never going to belong to *that* sort of world.

Yet time was passing and some drastic action was required.

Something.

Anything.

And with that thought, the tin pot vigorously shook itself, jumping up and down repeatedly on the shelf, and rattling so much that, beneath and below, on lower shelves, those other long forgotten items and utensils trembled and quivered.

"There was a time where I had RESPECT", shouted the tin pot. "A time where I had station in this world".

It peered once more over the edge of the shelf. And this time, even despite the gloom of the pantry, it managed to glimpse those other utensils ducking, shaking, hiding and what have you.

"Aha! AHA!" it shouted. Clearly, being enraged, having a tantrum, jumping loudly up and down on the shelf, was the way to get attention. Maybe even the best way. That old colander, two shelves down, for instance, was quite visibly upset.

"So that's it, is it?" said the pot to itself. "I'm supposed to sit here, forgotten with desiccated spiders for company and simply accept that? Do nothing? Fade away? Be turned into that bicycle? Well no, no! NO! Not me. Not this tin pot. I can still make an impact on this world. All I have to do is get mad, get angry, unleash my dark side. That will show them. All of them! And I'll take the whole pantry with me, if needs be".

And *that* was the point at which the old saucepan, the big tin pot, decided that some sort of pantry war, a cataclysmic grab for attention, was the only way forward.

War!

Bang!

Attack!

*That* was the way forward!

*That* was the way to get back on the table. To be filled with stews and onions and mashed potatoes again.

War! It was the obvious solution!

"You WEAKLINGS! Look at you all, down there, cowering there in the dark! Accepting your lot in life!"

How best to proceed though?

Ah, now that wasn't so easy.

Very few people bothered with the pantry, any more.

Everybody in the house, presumably, knew that there was nothing left inside the cupboard apart from a lot of broken down bits and bobs.

Nevertheless... nevertheless... from time to time the cupboard door, the pantry door, *was* still opened.

Only last summer, for instance, a snotty little brat had peered in looking for something called 'hiscaterpault'. It wasn't there. But he had picked up a few empty jam jars, and taken them away 'forsticklebacks'. Whatever they were.

And way back before that, dark and cold it had been, the pantry had briefly been home to a Christmas pudding.

The scents and smells from that had been wonderful. Like old times. And every broken utensil in the panty had leaned over, trying to see the pudding. Wondering, hoping, if this was the start of a new age. Of being put back into use again.

Alas no. The pudding had been removed only a day or so later and the pantry had fallen back into dark, cool and dreary neglect.

But at least it did prove that the opportunity existed. That the moment *could* arrive. Thus it was only a question of careful planning, and patience. Maybe lots of patience. Yes, but the time would come. One day, at some point in the future, that door would open.

And then?

The old tin pot rocked slightly from side to side. Humming to itself. The saucepanny equivalent of nodding its head.

When that day arrived, the saucepan would leap from the top shelf and make a dash for the kitchen door.

Yes! Yes, that was what it would do.

And *en route*, as it fell past the other shelves, it would make damned sure that it's handle, it's long old handle, caught hold of as many other pots, jam jars and plastic utensils as possible. Dragging the lot of them down as it fell.

That old sandwich maker. The pot would be sure to give *that* a clattering blow on the way past. How that thing once thought it was going to take over the world! The arrogance of it. In practice it had only ever been used once, before being abandoned in the pantry. Ha!

But... no.

Actually. No.

"But I'm a saucepan, for goodness sake, not a marathon runner", said the pot to itself. "Even if I do make it out the kitchen, I will surely get no further than the washing line in the back garden before one the dozen or so dogs in the house catch up with me".

"Yes, I could bash all those other things on the way out of this pantry. Give one or two of them a right old shiner! But I'd end up just as battered and bruised. And, what would I achieve? Nothing! I would either be gotten rid of or put back in here!"

And then, slowly, but surely, harsh reality began to dawn.

For all that it had once been a very important part of the household, for all that it had once been a major player in the kitchen, the truth was that the saucepan, the big, bold aluminium pot, was just that — an old saucepan.

And there was nothing sane it could do, to force the world to pay attention to it.

And there was nothing it could do to even get back into weekly use.

It had long since lost it's red lid.

It was out of fashion.

And nobody cared.

It was just an old tin pot, in a great big half-empty pantry, making a lot of noise and upsetting everybody else for no good reason.

# Paddington at home

"Hi, hello, how was your day, dear?" It was Mrs Paddington Bear who spoke. The front door to their little nook had just closed. Paddington Bear had just come home. It had been a very long day.

"Phew!" said Paddington, kicking off his yellow wellies and going into their tiny, but cosy kitchen, to greet his wife.

"Hello dear", he said, giving her a small kiss on her furry cheek.

"So how was it?" said Mrs Paddington, placing a big mug of tea and freshly made marmalade sandwiches in front of her husband. "How did it go?"

Paddington sighed again. "Well... to be quite honest, we got on very well. And I feel that it could make quite a splash in the newspapers and what have you, you know, if it is used properly".

"Oh that is good", said Mrs Paddington. "Then I will be able to see some piccies of the day and read all about it".

"Oh yes", said Paddington, taking a huge bite of his sandwich and, needless to say, getting marmalade all over his furry paws and cheeks as he did so. "But... you know, it really isn't me. It just isn't. I mean, all that grandeur, that opulence. The sheer weight of wealth inside that palace. It's bloody scandalous, in truth. And they've not only got that one home, they've got dozens of them". He took another bite of the sandwich, managing to get a big splodge of marmalade on the end of his nose. "You know me, I campaign for Shelter, for the homeless. And I did feel a proper traitor to those poor folk, sitting in that place and meeting her and scoffing all that food".

"Oh yes", said Mrs Paddington. "I understand dear. I do. I know it was difficult for you. But so long as it helps to raise the issue of homelessness, then it was all done for a good cause".

Paddington slowly nodded his rather large head. "Yessss", he said. "Yes. But you know... really... I am not so sure now. And I actually have the horrible feeling that they were only using me for free publicity and that they won't do anything at all about the homeless".

# Greenfingers

So here we are again, coming up to halfway through another year.

2022 seems to have moved along so very quickly, doesn't it?

And what a year it has been...

But first let me introduce myself... my name is Flourish. A little unusual, yeah, I get that. I like it though, and I think that my name has had a big influence on who I am as a person. On how I've developed into myself, really. I suppose I felt that I wanted to live up to a name like that, and from my earliest years I was always kind of unique, slightly quirky in terms of my appearance and my outlook on life. You see, my parents were a bit off the wall... so they were never going to give me a conventional name like Karen or Jenny. I think they liked the idea of being a bit quirky too, but ultimately... yeah, they were the same has everyone else. And, well, to cut a long story short, that was kind of how I ended up living alone, in London, and at a very young age.

London? Yes. I left home at sixteen and moved to the Capital where I lived with a friend, for a while. Her name, oddly, *was* Karen. Which maybe tells you something, I'm not sure? Either way, we lived a pretty hedonistic lifestyle for a few years, doing various jobs like working in night clubs and what have you. But... eventually... Karen felt home sick and that was the last I saw of her. But not me, no, I stayed on in London.

I did have a few relationships. Yes I did. Guys came and went, nothing very serious. And I continued to live a pretty wild life until, one day, I decided it was time to get serious, to return to further education and get a degree in something or other. You know the sort of thing. I felt I was getting older and I needed some sort of a plan.

Well, after three years of study, with all of those also spent in London, I finally gained a Degree in Design. And that was where the harsh realities of life imposed themselves upon me. How? Why? Well there just wasn't the well-paid design job waiting for me after graduating that I had expected. I tried. Sure I did. But in the end I found myself settling down to do the most uncreative and soul-destroying of jobs, working in a government office of all things. And that really was a dull, dull job. Long unsociable hours, too. But I got paid very well and most of my work colleagues were great people, so I endured it year after year after year...

During much of that time, to be honest, I continued to live a fairly carefree life, at least outside of work. And then it happened, it happened to me like it happened to everyone else, Covid struck.

Now that was in 2020, of course. But, somehow, that Pandemic was also the point at which I decided, once more, to re-evaluate my life. It gave me a shock, so to speak. A wake-up call.

Well, it didn't take me long to see that I needed to make some changes. Not least because, by now, I was entering my late forties. Basically, I was fine for money. But I was also single and, in many ways, I was kind of lonely...

So what did I do? Well, not being the sort of person to hang around, I dived straight in. I resigned from my job in London and I moved to Brighton on the south coast, for a complete change of scenery. That was the start. But more than that, I wanted romance. I had never really had the time, inclination or enthusiasm before to pursue a love life before. Not properly. Don't get me wrong I had a lot of attention from people, I was attractive and I turned heads. But mostly I wasn't interested in them. But now? The year 2022? I often thought about being with someone fabulous again. I would watch couples stroll along the sea front laughing, touching and holding hands and it made me feel sad because that was what I wanted. To share that joy and contentment with someone else. After spending the best part of five years or so on my own, yes, it was time to find that special someone again. I was ready to find love. I was looking good and feeling positive.

And this is where this strange but true tale really starts...

*

It was delightful being out of the city, and I felt happier than I had in many years, much more relaxed and at peace with myself. I just needed a job and some love in my life, so the pursuit of both began in earnest.

With regard to men, well, you can imagine... I had a few meetings with some rather dubious types. Dating sites, you know. They looked interesting from their profiles. One was considerable older than me, not that age is a deal breaker. He was very attractive, striking actually and unique. He had his own business which was great. We had a few dates and I thought to myself there may be potential of something long term with this person. Unfortunately, he wasn't ready for a relationship and was going through some sort of midlife crisis. That led me onto a few others... a gallery owner who didn't stop talking and a very large businessman who was a bit creepy, both of whom were completely unsuitable for me.

And my job? Well, quite suddenly, a good job opportunity did come my way. It was working at the local University in an administrative role. Maybe not as creative as I would have liked, but it would certainly suffice for the foreseeable future. I applied, got the post and settled into the situation very nicely.

Life, it seemed, was getting slowly back on track for me.

Then, one evening, there was a staff get together. It was supposed to involve games, nibbles and drinks on the lawn, but unfortunately the weather had other ideas. So everyone congregated in the bar instead, and I sat with my colleagues not really mixing with anyone else.

After a short while the weather improved a little, and it was decided people could go outside and play volleyball or some such activity that involved hitting something or other over a net. Not my kind of thing at all.

I declined to join-in, preferring to sit on my own and assuring everyone that I was perfectly happy.

The truth was that I had already decided to quickly finish my drink and head off home. I had done enough socialising for one day.

Anyway, I did finish that drink and started to head out of the bar when I heard a voice say, "Surely you're not leaving just yet?" I turned around, and at the far end of the bar sat a man, a very attractive man. Very. He was a similar age to me, I guess, with dark brown hair which was tousled and fell about his shoulders.

I asked him if he was speaking to me. "Of course," he replied, in a soft voice, "Come and join me if you like, it's too early to leave just yet". I was a little stunned by this sudden and unexpected but very welcome invitation.

And with that, he got up from his chair to invite me over.

I could see now that he was about six-foot-tall with an athletic build. He was wearing a black tailored jacket, with a very unusual looking flower in his lapel, a flower which I was inexplicably drawn to. Beneath the jacket he wore a grey tee shirt and black jeans. He wore black shoes. I like nice shoes and a sense of style. And this man had all of that without even trying. It was effortless, I could tell. Some people are fortunate that way, everything just seems to fall into place.

So, yeah, I joined him.

His name, ironically as you will soon see, was Professor Tobias Plant and he worked at the University in the Science department where he was involved in some secret experimentation involving fauna and flora and genetic modifications or GM, for short.

And I soon discovered that not only was he extremely attractive and rather engaging, but he was also single.

But there was something else, too; he had such a wonderful fragrant scent about him. I couldn't place it, but it was soft and subtle and made me feel relaxed and calm. Dreamy. You know.

Well... Anyway... As you might have guessed by now, Professor Plant and I spent the rest of that evening getting acquainted, we chatted and we flirted. He admitted noticing me a few weeks back when I first started working at the University. He shyly mentioned the fact he had been struck when he first saw me and he absolutely adored my name. He told me that he had been determined to introduce himself to me that evening, and that it was the perfect opportunity for our encounter. And then, abruptly, he took the strange little flower thing out of his jacket lapel and placed it delicately behind my ear.

I noticed immediately, of course, that it was the strange flower which produced the subtle scent I so adored.

Well... overall, it was the most perfect evening. We continued to chat and laugh at the silliest things and I admit I felt giddy and lightheaded.

Sadly, the end of the evening was then upon us. The bar was closing and we were the last people there. We finished our drinks and walked out into the cool night air. I felt refreshed and vibrant, which was strange after three full glasses of wine. That much wine would usually have the reverse affect.

The Professor walked me to a taxi and bent towards me, kissing my cheek, his tousled hair brushing against my face, tickling me.

And that was the end of a very special evening.

The next morning, a Saturday, I awoke thinking the Professor must have been part of a wonderful dream, but then I noticed something on my pillow — it was that strange looking plant. The one he had given me. I picked it up gently because it looked so fragile, it was like a delicate, spindly twig with tiny spines and a very small emerald flower and, most of all, it had that wonderful fragrance. I had never quite seen anything like that tiny flower before. It was mesmerising and I have to admit that I spent most of the weekend continually going back to the plant both to admire it and to rediscover that intoxicating scent.

Monday morning finally came around and I was full of excitement... sort of mixed up with anxiety. Not really knowing what to expect, or even if I would see the Professor again.

During the course of my day, I did a bit of discreet investigating with regard to the Professor. No one in my office knew much, if anything, about him and I couldn't even find his name or email address at the Science lab. So there was no way I could contact him. Was he perhaps some sort of fake? Not a real professor? That would be just typical of my luck. I thought he seemed too good to be true...

A few days more passed and I heard nothing and discovered nothing. And I began to feel resigned to never seeing the enigmatic Professor Plant again.

Then out of the blue, or rather out of the science lab, I had another encounter as I was heading out of the office on my way to the train. By now it was Friday and I wanted to get home and put this disappointing week behind me. Then I heard a voice shouting my name; "Flourish, hey Flourish It's Tobias, wait up".

I turned round and looked behind me and there, running toward me, was the Professor. His deep brown eyes sparkled as he embraced me.

He had missed me very much, he said, and couldn't wait to meet me again. He asked if I would like to go back to his house, it was near the campus, just the other side of the park.

I agreed and we walked slowly hand in hand to his home.

He told me he had been busy with work, so much to do but so little time.

We arrived at his place, a large detached Georgian house standing somewhat apart from the surrounding properties, on the edge of the park. A handsome building, he said it was owned by his family but that he was staying there on his own.

We went inside and he took me to the front room. It was very comfortable and well decorated, if a little untidy maybe.

We sat and chatted, he was next to me on the sofa.

We enjoyed a glass or two of delicious wine, talking mostly about the things we felt passionate about. His real concern was the environment, and he felt sure that his work was hopefully going to improve things in the future. But he couldn't say too much about it at this time.

I was also keen on environmental issues, so we talked about these more serious topics and the time once again just flew by. By now, it must have been approaching midnight. and I yawned, I couldn't help myself. It had been an ordinary day that had turned out to be so very perfect and unexpected. I was tired. I admit it. So I got up from the sofa to fetch my jacket, and said to him that it was time I went home.

Tobias stood up, too, and told me he wanted me to stay with him. He couldn't let me go again. He needed to be with me. And, in all honesty, I also felt the desire to be with him.

Now you must understand I wouldn't normally spend the night with a virtual stranger on just the second date, but I couldn't resist. I really didn't want to be away from this man.

Well... as you can imagine... we spent the night together. A most wonderful and intoxicating night. And we both drifted off the sleep in each other's arms.

I stayed with Tobias all the following day, I only had the same clothes I had worn to work the previous day, but none of that mattered. I borrowed a jumper and some jogging bottoms.

We talked all day, it's funny because our conversation again just flowed, it was so easy and so very right. I told him about my life but still didn't know much about him. From my understanding, however, he worked on a privately funded project at the University. Something to do with plants and experimentation to help improve the environment. All hush hush stuff, he still couldn't say too much.

I returned home the next day. I hated being away from Tobias, but he assured me that he would see me again in a few days time.

Once at home I relaxed and recollected my time with this intriguing man. I had never known such intensity of feeling and it occurred to me I was already in love.

The following week, and I was back at work not expecting to hear or see Tobias for a few days.

But I missed him terribly, so I decided I would visit him in his laboratory. He had told me that it was located on the outer perimeter somewhere, in a remote part of the Science complex. An experimental place. Hidden. Forgotten. A bit of both. Which was why he had no contact details.

I wasn't sure what to expect when I arrived at his lab.

It seemed quiet.

Very quiet.

And there was nobody around.

I knocked on the door. But there was no answer.

So I decided to be brave and let myself in.

Once inside it was surprisingly dark and all I could hear were faint rustling noises. "Tobias are you there, it's Flourish, are you OK?"

But there was no reply.

For a moment, I thought about leaving. But no, instead of doing that, I went further into the laboratory, flicking a switch which abruptly lit the place up.

And what an amazing sight it was!

The room was an abundance of foliage, like some sort of fantastical botanical interior. All sorts of plants. Things I had never seen before and could not begin to name. But over and above all of that, everywhere I turned, there were more of those little emerald green flowers. Dozens of them. Perhaps even hundreds. And there, too, was that heady smell again, the scent, the fragrance of those little flowers, only now, in this room, it was so much more pungent that it overcame me, and I felt faint, trembling and totally overwhelmed. I was even sure, for a moment, that I was going to pass out.

But then, quite suddenly, I felt myself being shaken to my senses. It was Tobias; "Flourish, please, it's me, are you alright?"

I could hear panic in his voice. I lost my balance and fell into his arms. And I started muttering incoherently, trying to apologise for entering his domain without being invited.

He whispered, "Don't worry I'm here. I love you Flourish".

Well.... I think that is when I lost consciousness. I came around sometime later, and found myself in an office, lying on a small sofa tucked away at the back of the room, behind a large desk.

"Where am I?" I said. Or some words to that effect.

"Here", said Tobias, passing me what he assured me was simply a glass of whisky, "Drink this".

I drank it.

And that was when I noticed something very odd about Tobias. He now had a little growth on his hands and around his neck, they looked like hairs but were thicker and seemed to be almost sprouting from him like branches on a tree or stalks on a plant.

I started. He saw that, saw my worry, my concern, my fear. "Don't be scared Flourish", he said softly, "Nothing will hurt you. There is only love for you here. I am something more than you can understand now, but it will all become clear very soon. Very soon".

Well... my head swam, but I wasn't scared and he was right, I did slowly become aware of so much more.

It appeared that Tobias, the professor, my professor, had discovered the emerald flower whilst undertaking research into the genetic engineering of plants.

One afternoon, whilst working, he had cut himself on one of the tiny spines which the little plants possessed.

Only a little scratch. But it had been enough.

Enough to fuse his human DNA with that of the plant.

"Those little flowers, those plants, they know we are ruining this world", said Tobias, his voice sounding distant, rustling almost, just like leaves blowing in a gentle breeze. "Humans will never be able to stop making war, stop killing one another, stop all their destruction...".

He moved closer to me. By now, or was I imagining it, his hair was foliage. Leaves. And I suppose at that moment I should have been scared. Terrified even. But I wasn't. I was transfixed and unable to move. I felt heady, that same scent again. So strong. So wonderful.

It all felt right. Just right. Perfect.

"And so we shall replace humanity. We shall take control of the world before it is too late. Save the planet from them".

"We?"

"Yes".

And that was how it all began.


It had been the whisky, of course. It had not been alcohol. It had contained the results of his most recent experiments. And I had swallowed it. Every drop of it.

And even as Tobias told me about the emerald flowers, I could feel myself changing. Changing and understanding more.

"We can begin again", he said quietly, calmly. "A new world order. Better. Kinder. A new Adam, half man, half plant. And you, Flourish, you shall be my Eve, a new Eve...".

# Take everything away

It had taken Tina and Alan over 3 years to save the deposit
for their first time buy — a tiny, cramped one bed flat,
which backed onto a busy railway line, which had a chip-
shop (called Lardies) for one neighbour and what was
delicately called a 'problem family' as the other neighbour.
A problem family? You know the sort, one of those homes
with lots of old broken cars in the front garden, and lots of
rubbish in the back and a seemingly endless line of scooters

delivering pizzas and burgers. A family who blamed immigrants for everything but never really worked for themselves. *That* sort of family.

But... yes... at least, at last, Tina and Alan were on the property ladder.

Not that it is a ladder. Not really. That's just one of those daft, empty expressions which are used to try to encourage folk to 'Carry On Regardless'. The reality is, without someone else dying in a very timely manner and leaving you a lot of cash, there was no real way off the first rung. So, as a ladder, even if it was a ladder, because it generally had only one rung, it was a pretty useless ladder!

However. Tina and Alan had, finally, made it.

They would no longer be paying an extraordinarily large fortune in rent, only a relatively small fortune via an overly extended mortgage.

But they had done it.

They had their *own place*.


Sadly, however, I need to wind back a bit here. Because, and it's a thing that seems peculiar to our modern world, lots of stories can only be told with a little bit of scene setting first.

Because our world today isn't a straightforward one full of kings and queens, princes turned into frogs or giants, nor one filled with home made chutney, tadpoles in jam jars, Will Hay films, wardrobes, witches and lions. No. We have made a right old tangle of things in recent decades and our lives have become needlessly complicated, difficult and stress-filled.

And we have done that with most things.

Pretty much everything, in fact.

And whilst each country — like each person, each job, each life — has it's good points and it's upsides (for they *all* do), so too does everything and everywhere and everyone have it's fair share of bad points and downsides (for they *all* have that, as well). And housing is one of the things which the UK does badly at.

Very, very, badly at.

Why so?

Well here is the aforementioned 'little bit of scene-setting' which, really, is unavoidable: a long time ago... way back in the late 1940s, government had the laudable idea of trying to build a more equal nation. The Second World war had ended, but it had left behind a good deal of rubble-strewn wasteland, unemployment and shattered dreams. And the country needed a lift. More than a lift, it needed a change of direction. A new start. A boost. Socially, economically and in terms of morale.

How to achieve that new start? Government decided that three key elements were required: decent healthcare, job security and affordable homes. And all three of those things were to be offered to everybody. Absolutely everybody.

And it made good sense.

It really did.

For when you build with a solid foundation, you can build something that is truly worth having.

On the other hand... if you skimp on that foundation, or choose to cut it away... then things tend to collapse. And unfortunately, after 30 or so good years post-war, on or about May 1979, that very 'cutting away' began.

And it began in earnest.

And men, and women, regardless of political persuasion, have ever since continued to do that sorry cutting.

Needless to say, then, that the new start, the better Britain which the generation who survived two world wars began to build... has now, somewhat, crumbled away.

And it has crumbled away most of all, in the area of housing.

Long gone is the idea that everyone (in such a chilly and damp country!) needs or deserves a roof over their head.

Long gone, too, is the idea that homes should be affordable or even remotely affordable.

Housing, as any honest person will tell you, is the real cancer at the core of British society today.

Now there *was* a reason, a very real, very nasty reason for making housing so unaffordable. It was all about security, job security, security of family, of home and community. There were some people who did not want ordinary folk to have all of those things and those same people finally tricked — for that is what they did — others into voting for their nasty ideas.

And from that point on, house prices — not just for the poorest but for everyone — rocketed. And, in many parts of the country, having a home, certainly a decent home, has become an unobtainable dream.

That much, of course, is established political history.

But as to why others since, left, right and centre, have come and gone and done nothing about the situation... well, that is anybody's guess.

So this story, then, which is about a carpet, in a way, begins in a country where housing is no longer a given and where little organisations have, in places, taken it upon themselves to provide some, a bit, a few, a smidgen of cheap social housing.

Now some of these organisations do a very good job. That should be made clear straight away. And those folk actually put the needs of their tenants first. They really do.

But too many of those organisations, or housing associations as we should properly call them, put money and profit first instead. They know that the poorest 10 percent, 20 percent or even 30 percent of the country struggle to get adequate housing. And they know that those same folk live in fear, constant fear, of 'doing wrong', of 'breaking some rules', and of being evicted and turfed out onto the street.

They can, sad to say, do almost what they like with their tenants.

So... now the scene, for this story, is well and truly set... because Tina and Alan, were moving *out* of a property which belonged to a housing association and *into* the aforementioned flat 'of their own'.


"It's funny", said Tina as the two of them sat, one evening, watching TV after a long, hard day at work. "Only three months ago, we still felt a mile off our own place. Remember?"

Alan picked up the remote control, muted the volume on the TV and turned to Tina.

"We'd been saving forever and with house prices going up and up, it just felt as if we would never be out of this place".

Alan nodded. Inadvertently glancing around their flat as he did so. This particular flat, belonged to the housing association. It would be another week or so before they could move out. "Yes", he said. "Then my Mom died, and we got the extra money we needed for our deposit".

It was sad, but true. For as mentioned above, often, you needed a dear one to die in order to be able to afford a home of your own. How had the world come to this?

"Yes", said Tina. Lightly touching Alan's hand. "I'm sorry, darling".

Alan shrugged. He had been very close to his mom, but he knew how the world was, how things worked. She would have been happy to see him, and Tina, use the money to move into their own place.

Only even then, with *her* death, there still had not been enough for a deposit. Not quite enough.

Prices just kept on going up, and up, and up. And up, and up and up.

Fortunately — if it is not inappropriate to use that word — Tina's father had died the very next week. Possibly, so they thought, as a result of the shock of Alan losing his mother. The two families being very close.

And that extra cash, from the father's death, had been enough, just about, to afford the deposit.

"I wish we could wind the clocks back a little, though", said Alan.

Tina didn't reply, but kept hold of Alan's hand.

"You know, this last year, if we could have done a few things differently".

"I know", said Tina gently. "Perhaps if we had realised how ill your mom was...".

Alan shook his head. "No. No, I don't mean that. No. We are born, we all have to die. No, I mean this place. This flat".

Tina frowned. "What do you mean?"

"Well", said Alan, "Look at the carpet in this one room. It's wall to wall. And fitted. Properly fitted. And only six months old. We felt so sure that we would never get the other together, the deposit I mean, that we decided to spend a little bit on this place. And although we can take some of the stuff with us, to the new flat, the carpets... well, they won't fit. The rooms are entirely different sizes and shapes. And the same is true of the curtains too. These would be too short for our new place, with it's older and bigger windows".

"Oh, yes", said Tina, looking around the room almost as if seeing it for the first time. "Yes. Of course. I hadn't even thought of that".

"And the tall fridge-freezer", said Alan. "Even that. I don't think it will fit well under the low ceiling of the new place. It is quite pokey in there, in that respect".

"Ah, no, that will be OK", said Tina. "We can give that to my brother. That won't go wasted".

Alan nodded. That was good to hear. But the other stuff? The carpets, curtains, even the work which had been done in terms of painting the place, and putting up some wallpaper recently, none of that could come to the new flat? What of all that?

"Wait, though!" said Tina, sitting up a bit. "It will be fine. Good in fact. Remember when we first moved here and we had no money? We didn't have a carpet of any kind for months. Not even a mat. Nothing".

"No. No, we did", said Alan. "Remember? The rules of the Housing Association are that every room must be carpeted. So we had to take out a loan for carpet".

"Oh yes", said Tina. "Of course, I had forgotten that. Yes. But that makes what I am saying even better, then!"

Alan frowned and then yawned. It had been a long day and, really, it was time for bed. "It does?"

"Yes", said Tina. "We can leave all these carpets, and all the curtains, leave them behind for the new people. The people who move in here after we leave. You can be sure they will be a young couple or even a single mom, and they will be short of money. They have to be desperately poor to get a place like this. From a housing association".

"Oh yes!" said Alan, leaning towards Tina and giving her a soft kiss on the cheek. "What a great idea! Of course. That would make a great present for them. Well done!"

"I am not working tomorrow", said Tina. "I will go and speak to the Association about it. Tell them what we have decided to do".

And, with that matter settled, the two of them went to bed. Feeling a good deal happier about the carpets and the curtains and, rightly, feeling they were doing others a good turn.

"No". The French have a very emphatic way of saying 'no'. And it is the standard response whenever you make any attempt to communicate with one of their billions and billions of bureaucrats.

In Britain, the same word is, typically, pronounced less often and with a markedly less inflexible tone.

However, on this occasion, the word 'no' was being used with the full French-style vigour. And it was being used by Mrs Gail Kerrigan-Brown, head of the Newfields Housing Association. And it was being used, as you may have guessed by now, in response to Tina's suggestion that she and Alan leave behind carpets and curtains for the new, incoming tenants.

"No". she said again. "Most definitely not. No".

Most people work all their lives, because they don't have any choice in the matter. But some people work as a way of filling their empty days. They already live in a very large detached house, with a gravel drive, own at least two brand new Range Rovers, plus a BMW, plus a vintage car, they already have a substantial income from 'other sources', their partner is 'self-made' and ruthless with it and, really, given their starkly apparent personality disorders, they would do better to 'fill those empty days' by staying indoors, well out of the way of the rest of the world for whom, evidently, they had very little time.

Mrs Gail Kerrigan-Brown was one of the latter. The sort of soul who would run a little shop in one of the remotest corners of the Peak District, selling ladies underwear at double High Street Chelsea prices. The sort of soul who would then complain about the lack of sales, complain about hikers being 'scruffy sorts', insist the public footpath which touched the corner of her property was re-routed, and who also took her holidays (at least four a year) in the most expensive, but never the most exclusive, of sun-kissed resorts.

Only, in this instance, Gail K-B had not opted for such a 'petite boutique' in the higher parts of Derbyshire. No. She had flicked a coin between opening an adoption agency ("the money to be made there has to be seen to be believed") or showing some sign, however vague, of social conscience by opening a small housing association ("the money to be made there has to be seen to be believed").

And it had been the housing association which had 'come up Heads'.

"Absolutely not. No". she said again. "Everything must be taken out. You knew that when you became one of our tenants and it is made clear to you every year, when the new rules and regulations are issued".

"Yeah... but...", said Tina, hopefully, "But surely rules... rules can be bent or broken. I mean, in this case, the stuff is all new and we would be helping some younger folk... some of your new tenants".

"No", said Gail K-B again. "I set the rules in this association. Nobody else. And my rules clearly state that tenants, when leaving, must, in all circumstances, remove everything when they leave a property vacant".

"But the carpets are new".

"No".

"The curtains too".

"No. No! You have to take everything away".

Tina shook her head. "Everything?"

"Yes! Everything. And I will tell you this for free... if you don't remove the lot, and I mean *the lot*, then you will have to pay, as it says in the rules, any and all removal costs which we will then have to incur on your behalf. Plus cleaning costs".

Again, Tina shook her head. "And those... how much would those be?"

Gail K-B scowled at Tina. But that was nothing personal as she scowled at everyone. For despite being loaded, expensively dressed, very well-manicured and so forth, she was a singularly unpleasant character.

"It is in the rules. All of it. It is all in the rules".

Tina shrugged.

"Removal costs are charged at 275 pounds per hour. Minimum charge four hours. And I think you'll find that cleaning costs are much the same".

Now although it had taken Tina and Alan a long time to save their deposit for their new flat, they were not stupid. Not thick. Nothing like that. There is a common misconception that the 'best people' get the highest salaries. But that is nonsense. What you get, in this world, depends almost entirely on *who* you know — not *what* you know. So Tina was more than capable of doing a quite bit of arithmetic. "275 pounds per hour? So that would be... what... over two thousand pounds? Two grand for a bit of cleaning and taking a few carpets and curtains out? That's daylight robbery!"

The Kerrigan-Browns had made their money from bullying and building, in equal measure, and it showed.

"Those are the rules", said Gail K-B. "You must remove everything. Or else".

"OK", said Tina, an idea taking shape in her head. "OK. Well, I think you are a bloody crook. And I think your rules stink. And, what is more, in this day and age, I think what you are doing is a scandalous waste of resources and materials. To throw out new carpets and curtains, then to insist your new tenants fit carpets and curtains even where that means going into debt... it's criminal".

"Those are *the rules*", said Gail K-B. "Everything has to be taken out. Is that clear?"

"Yes", said Tina. "Perfectly".


There is an old saying, a wise one, that you should never tackle a stranger in the street. They may look harmless, they may look thin and weedy, but even the scrawniest of men could be carrying a gun, or a knife or else they may have four or five very large friends nearby.

The same is true — or it should be true — in all walks of life: be nice to other people, be kind, give a little, give a lot, bend the rules if needs be and help make the world a better place. Either that or leave folk well alone.

And so it was, two weeks later that Gail Kerrigan-Brown squeezed her huge four wheel drive into two of the allotted parking spaces outside the home where Alan and Tina used to live.

And she was, once again, in a foul mood.

Alan and Tina had completed their own purchase, and moved out, a few days beforehand. Leaving the keys and signed paperwork for the Association's flat with Gail K-B's secretary.

Now the fact that the secretary had allowed them to do that, in Gail's absence, had infuriated her. The secretary, a nice young chap, had been fired on the spot. "It's a rule. A rule", she had screamed at the secretary. "We never, ever, allow tenants to leave one of our properties before they have been thoroughly inspected. By accepting their keys, and signing them out, we have... or, rather, *you* have... effectively said that they have no legal liability over the condition of that property. So you are fired. Right here and now. And when I go around, personally, to inspect the place, God help you if I find that the property needs cleaning or anything".

That was the sort of mood she was in. As ever.

And as she stepped out of her vast car, other frightened tenants who were simply popping out to the shops or chatting to friends in the car park, almost cowered away from her.

She glowered around at them, all of them, and then strode purposefully to Number 38C, the flat where Alan and Tina used to live.

"Better be the right damn key", she said as she fumbled around in her sillily expensive handbag to find the thing.

She found the key.

Put it in the lock.

And turned the thing.

The door opened.

It *was* the right key. So at least that was something.

Then she took the key out of the lock, put in back in her handbag and pushed the front door open.

And as she did that, her jaw dropped. Dropped low enough, almost, to touch her toes.

There was a front door. Yes.

There were windows on the front of the property. Yes.

There was the front wall, too. Yes.

But beyond those things? There was nothing. Nothing at all. Not a thing. Only a blank and wholly empty space where there had once been a flat. And beyond that? A rather pleasant view across to the park, where some little children were playing football.

Because everything had been taken away. Exactly as the 'rules' had demanded.

# Just like 1976

The sun blazed down. Day after day. Just as it had done now for so long. So very long. How long exactly? That was hard to say. The days had become weeks. The weeks had become months. That much was certain. No rain. Blue skies. Sun. Sun and heat. Because it was hot, too. Very hot. Day after day after day after day...

And everywhere you went, it was the same story: dried up streams, rivers low on water, hosepipe bans, yellowed and straw coloured fields, no sign of greenery, not really, not any more. Office blocks were too hot. Shops were even hotter. Using the bus, or the train was no fun at all, patience was short, tempers were frayed.

Heatwave.

The world being cooked alive.

And Sarah knew all that. Knew it well. Because she had the misfortune to commute, every day, from the south coast and into London and back, for her work. And that commute, with those stressed folk, hot trains, through that desiccated countryside made for a pretty depressing, daily, experience.

However, Sarah did have one thing going for her; once back home, with her husband Jack, she could relax. Relax because they were fortunate enough to have a nice house, set in a fairly sheltered position, which for many hours each day provided cool shade, away from the worst of the heat and the sun. And to finish that commute each day... to get back home... with Jack already there (for he worked much closer to home and finished before Sarah) and to find him in the garden, with a long cool drink ready for her, helped Sarah to get through the worst of it all.

"Hi, Jack, I'm back", she called, as she walked through the front door. So relieved to feel it close, heavily, behind her. Shutting the rest of the exhausted world out.

Sarah kicked off her shoes, dropped her bag and went to find Jack.

The two of them met, in the hall, sort of half-way between the front door and the kitchen.

Jack, however, was frowning. Clearly something was awry.

"What is it?" asked Sarah.

Jack nodded over his shoulder. "My dad's here. Sorry".

Sarah felt her spirits sink.

In most respects Bill, aged seventy, was a nice enough man. Honest, fit and active, with a good pension and a home of his own. Lots of interests too. Always busy. Yes, a nice enough man. But in some respects... a bit less so. A bit, to be blunt, of a gammon, as the expression went.

"Where is he?" she said, quietly.

"In the garden".

"I'll pop out and say hello".

"Thanks, love. I know what he can be like. I'll bring you a drink out".

So Sarah went out into the back garden, via the French windows, to where a white iron table stood together with four or five matching iron seats, under a deeply shaded garden umbrella. And, sure enough, already there with an iced drink in his hand, was Bill.

"Hi Bill", said Sarah, trying hard to sound more enthusiastic than she felt. "Hot again".

As soon as she said those last two words, she knew they were a mistake. She only said them out of politeness, matter of factness, something to say.

"Hello, Sarah", said Bill, placing his glass down on the table, his face a little red from the sun. "Hmm... I suppose so. But we had it hot too, you know, back in 1976".

Inside, Sarah sighed. Hugely. How many times had he told them that? Every single time the hot weather was mentioned, every single time the word 'climate' came up in conversation, Bill made reference to 1976.

"Yes", she said. "I know. I know you did, Bill. I know. But, be fair, it is Christmas in two days time".

# Doubting Thomas

Thomas had been a happy little boy. An only child, yes, but quite content to be without brothers and sisters. After all, as an infant, that had meant lots of extra attention, with love and adoration being truly showered upon him by his doting mother and father.

At school, he had lots of chums. He was liked, likeable and studious. Not for Thomas smoking behind the bike sheds, carrying on with girls or playing truant. Oh no, no. Thomas was a good boy.

And when he hit his teenage years, he still studied hard, gained good exam results and went into college, much to the admiration of his very proud parents. Always happy and with a positive outlook on life, he remained well liked and made many more friends, sailing through his days in a protected bubble, mostly oblivious to any harm or hurtful encounters.

After three years at college, and having obtained a first-class degree, it was then time for Thomas to enter the adult world of work. And this he did. With ease. He found a suitable work position with a lot of prospects for promotion.

The next step? To move out of home, of course, and into his own flat or apartment and so become a truly independent young man.

All in all, a rather perfect start to life.

Unfortunately, time always passes. And the world can be an unpredictable sort of place and, sooner or later, a hard knock or two are sure to arrive and turn even the most blissful life on its head.

And that was precisely what happened to Thomas...

Firstly, over the course of a few years, whilst Thomas was still new to his flat and doing very nicely, his parents began to have marital problems. And emotional problems. And financial problems. And health problems.

For a start, though now comfortably in his mid-fifties, his father had become unhappy in his job, couldn't cope with mounting pressures and had lost an important promotion of his own to a younger colleague. From there, more or less, he had turned to drink to drown his disappointment, gambled heavily in secret and ran up huge amounts of debt. And then, in order to pay off the money he had loaned from some very dubious and dangerous money lenders, he embezzled large amounts of cash from the company he worked for.

Eventually Thomas's father got discovered for his embezzling and the whole sordid story was exposed to the world. It ended up with him being charged and found guilty. And he was thrown in prison a few years for his crimes. His wife — Thomas' mother — was disgusted by all of it, and soon divorced him after the humiliation of his criminal and debauched ways became public knowledge.

For Thomas, needless to say, all of this stuff was pretty devastating. But by the time he found out about it, most of it, it was already much too far gone and there was very little he could do to help. (Sadly, such is often the case with troubles like these). And that, I suppose, his inability to help his parents, was perhaps the key reason for the change in Thomas' previously good, happy and easy-going character.

Slowly, but surely, from this point on he became sullen and withdrawn. And instead of always being positive he became pessimistic and doubtful. For Thomas it was never "if" bad things were going to happen, but "when" they were going to happen.

And these changes effected his relationship with his girlfriend. Before all this happened, he knew that she loved him, but now he doubted this. He thought she was being unfaithful and why not? Look at what had happened to his own wonderful parents. So Thomas became jealous and eventually drove his girlfriend away onto the arms of another.

Friends saw it, too. He wasn't that fun and happy go lucky guy anymore. He always seemed serious and miserable. He would drink too much on nights out, get loud and confrontational, more often than not getting into scuffles and usually coming off the worst for it.

And, finally, even his work saw it. Instead of being the man that would excel and go places Thomas just coasted along, often even turning up late. Thomas got warned about his behaviour and attitude, of course he did, but he ignored all the advice and carried on regardless. And, ultimately, he was passed over for a prestigious promotion and told the boss to "stick it" and found himself unemployed and on the dole.

Long gone was the bright, happy and sheltered start he'd had to life.

The world in 2022 felt like a miserable, sort of place to be.

Until, one dark night, an extraordinary thing happened....


Thomas was making his way home after a long session roaring and scuffling down the pub.

Stumbling and grumbling as drunks tend to do, he cursed the pavement as he tripped on that, cursed a dog for having left a little brown gift behind, then cursed the sky for being black and the night for being cold.

Then he heard a strange, strange noise.

Very close by.

What was it?

It was loud, yes. And, in fact, it was a mobile phone ringing. But a strange ring tone, eerie, spacey, ethereal. Something he had certainly never heard before.

The ringing mesmerised him.

He stopped the stumbling and grumbling and cursing and looked around to see where the magical ringing sound was coming from.

But there was no one around. Not a soul.

Then, suddenly, and directly in front of him on the pavement, he saw the source of the sound: it was a shiny gold mobile phone, lying directly in his path.

Thomas swayed. Peered. Swayed again.

"Someone must have dropped it", he mumbled to himself. "Oh, well, not my business".

And so he continued on his way home. Staggering a little as he went.

A hundred metres further on, and the same noise.

The same astral sound. Only, somehow, more urgent, more pressing this time. More persistent. More definite.

Thomas stopped. Shook his head.

"Whassat?" he said.

And there, again, on the pavement in front of him, lay a gold mobile phone.

"Isnot my phone", he said to himself. "Is for you".

He laughed, shrugged and, once more, he walked on.

Well. This happened a few times. Until on or about the sixth or seventh occasion, he finally bent down and picked up the shiny gold mobile.

The ringing now louder than ever.

"Hello, who izz this, I know who you are, who are you? Whatdoyouwant?" asked Thomas.

A quiet voice, almost a whisper, replied. Asking politely if this was indeed Thomas on the phone.

Thomas did that thing with his head that drunks tend to do. A sort of double-take. "Wassss? Yeah. Yes. This is he, me. What do you want? Stop messing around... I am not in the slightest slightest bit amused by any of this. Go away and leave me alone. Me alone. I am throwing this mobile into the next river, or canal, or ducky pond, pond, pond, and that will be the end of your mischief once and for all".

The voice replied "No. No! Don't do that. I am your 'Three Wishes App'. You have become a doubter. You no longer believe in life and all the wonders it has to offer. So I am going to give you the chance to change your outlook again, to go back and be happy, become that person you once were. It's entirely up to you, of course, if you want to believe in change and the gift that I can offer you. But I will grant you three wishes. All you have to do is keep this mobile phone with you. And you will see how life can be good again".

And with that, the caller hung up.

Of course, Thomas knew he had maybe drunk more than he ought - which he had. And he doubted anything good would come of this business. But all the same, he put the mobile in his pocket just to be on the safe side.

And the following morning Thomas was awoken rather early by the strange ring tone again.

"Thomas is that you?" the voice asked.

"Yes, it is what do you want?" said Thomas, having more or less forgotten the events of the night before. "Who is that?"

The voice replied "Remember me? I am the 'Three Wishes App'. I can grant you three wishes to better yourself, to make yourself happy again, whatever, whatever it is that you desire. Anything. What is your first wish?"

Thomas, feeling a bit hung over from the night before, and not the happiest of souls at the best of times, thought for a moment. Was this just someone playing a prank? A joke of some sort? Maybe it was. But, what the hell, he would go along with it for amusement, to find some way of getting his own back on whoever it was.

"Alright then", he said, "I want promotion at work. Major promotion. Big time. I was passed by before, but it is long overdue".

With that the voice replied, "So be it" and abruptly hung up.

Thomas sat up in bed. Wondering what the devil was going on. Was that it? What on earth was the point of that? If it was a joke, it wasn't remotely funny.

Then his own phone rang. Not the special golden one, but his own rather scratched, worn and run-down mobile.

"Hello? Who is it?"

"Hi, Thomas? It's Mat from work. Listen, we've been having a bit of a think, and, well, we feel we made a mistake by-passing you for promotion, and that probably sent you off the rails a bit. And, well, to come to the point, we'd like to offer you a role as Senior Partner in the firm. How do you feel about that?"

Thomas frowned. Obviously the whole thing was some sort of practical joke. And although the voice on the phone did sound like Mat, one of the other Senior Partners at the firm, it was obviously just somebody doing an impersonation and taking the mickey out of Thomas.

"What do I think of that?" said Thomas. "Get stuffed! That is what I think of that! Stick your lousy job!"

The line went dead. Unsurprisingly. And, for a while, the world fell silent.

Thomas got up. Tripped over some clothes, carelessly discarded the night before. Got soap in his eyes, in the shower. Over-cooked the water for his coffee, making it both tasteless and scalding his mouth and then, once more, the golden phone rang. That same, ethereal, angelic ring tone.

"Thomas is that you?" the voice asked.

"Yes, it is! Who are you? What do you want", growled Thomas.

The voice replied "Remember me? I am the 'Three Wishes App'. I can grant you three wishes to better yourself, to make yourself happy again, whatever, whatever it is that you desire. Anything. What is your second wish?"

"My second wish?" For a moment Thomas was sorely tempted to say (though not in such polite words) 'I wish you'd go away and leave me alone', but he didn't say that and, instead, for whatever reason, found himself muttering "I wish I had my girlfriend back".

No sooner had he spoke, than his other phone, his own, ordinary mobile phone rang.

"H, Tom? It's me, Debbie. Listen, I've been thinking. You were under a lot of pressure when we broke up, and I should have stood by you. I see that now. What say we meet up, this evening, after work, and go for a drink? I'd love to have you back, if that is what you want".

Well, Thomas was furious by now. He didn't, for one moment, believe that it really was Debbie on the phone, though it did sound a bit like her, and so instead of agreeing to make a date, to meet up, put things back together again, he simply (if somewhat colourfully) told the person on the other end of the line to do something along the lines of take a running jump.

And after he had said that? Well, needless to say, the line went quite definitely dead.

"I've had enough of this nonsense", said Thomas to himself. "People got nothing better to do that make up all of this rubbish. Play jokes. Mess with my life. I bet I know who is behind all of this. And, what's more, I shall go round to their office, right now, and have it out with them. The swine".

He dropped and broke his coffee mug. Swore at the mess on the kitchen floor. Trod in a bit of doggy-log as soon as he set foot outside. Forgot a coat, even though it was raining hard. And made his wet, furious way to the nearest bus stop.

But... before he got there... that golden phone rang again.

That enchanting, dreamy, heavenly and blissful tone.

"Who the bloody hell is this?" yelled Thomas, as he answered the thing.

"Thomas is that you?" the voice asked.

"Yes, it is! You know it is! I'll swing for you! Why are you doing this? What do you want?"

The voice replied "Remember me? I am the 'Three Wishes App'. I can grant you three wishes to better yourself, to make yourself happy again, whatever, whatever it is that you desire. Anything. What is your third and final wish?"

Up ahead, and serenely approaching the bus stop, Thomas could see his bus. "What do I want? My third and final wish?"

The bus was coming. Thomas didn't have time to collect his thoughts. Not really.

"I'll tell you what, Mister bloody Three Wishes App or whatever you call yourself. My third wish? Go on then, I dare you, drop... drop a bloody great elephant out of the sky. Onto me. Right here. Right now".

And with those words, the line went dead.

But there was, needless to say, a sudden whistling sound. From somewhere overhead. A noise which seemed to be getting closer and closer and closer. Like the rapid approach of something or other.

Though long before Thomas ever reached his bus, that same sound had abruptly stopped. Replaced by a very heavy splatting and squelching noise.

# Excerpts from Boris' autobiography

I was born Alexander Boris 'Winston' de Piffle Johnson, on 19th June 1964. And I shall come back to that rather infamous date in a jiffy. But first, a word about the De Piffle part of my name, because folk often ask me about that.

In fact it's quite a funny story, really: a great grandfather of mine owned a fair bit of land. As you can probably imagine. And on that land, he had a few dozen peasant types eking out a pretty raw sort of living. Now their lives were hard. Yes they were. And I'd be the first to admit that. But their penury did help establish the wealth of my own family, which just goes to show that there are silver linings to every cloud. And to celebrate that acquisition of yet more wealth, that same grandfather invented the expression *'de piffle'*.

How? Why? What did it mean? Well, to put it briefly, whenever one of his impoverished tenants came to him, to plead their case in some respect or other, the old fellow simply did not want to speak to them. That wasn't because he was too busy or anything like that, but rather because he regarded the poor as some sort of low-life. So when they tried to engage him in conversation, along the lines of, "Oh dear Lord Johnson, our crops have failed again, I cannot afford to pay my rent. Please may we have more time to blah blah blah" or whatever, his terse reply was invariably "De Piffle".

It was a nonsensical word, of course. But, basically, it meant F... Off.

Then he would set the dogs on the tenant in question and, sometimes, give them both barrels of a shotgun, too.

Great fun!

The even funnier thing was that whenever he told us that story, he would invariably say it though a large mouthful of cake and brandy – the two mixed gummily together – and crumbs would go everywhere as he guffawed the words out.

And so, ever since his time, my family have kept those words, De Piffle, as part of our name. In part to remind us that we are incredibly rich, and in part to give us a chuckle or two at those who are not.

Of course these days we no longer set the dogs on the poor. No, no, we simply tax them far too much and con them left, right and centre. It has the same effect, really. Keeps them in their place. What?

......

......

......

But then a nanny arrived in my world who changed my way of looking at things.

Nanny Bob, we named her. And she played rugby.

So impressive was Nanny Bob that I actually began to pay attention to lessons, too. Yes. Even me. Not the easy stuff either, but the tough stuff like spelling my own name and counting up to and even just past 1.

Spiffing stuff, eh?

Another year or two must have passed before we realised that Nanny Bob was actually a chap. Yes, she, or he, dressed like a gal. So although, like all good Nans, she baked a mean spotted dick, underneath the wig and rollers and blue frock there was... well... an altogether different sort of dessert.

At first, because she was such a good old sort, we didn't mind that Nanny Bob was a man. In fact, if anything, it seemed like a 'two for the price of one' sort of thing as, at weekends, she could give us a bit of rugger practice. And, my goodness, she could punt oval balls a helluva long way. Got me well into the game.

Ah! But that was where it all went wrong for poor Nanny Bob.

One weekend, we had some jolly visitors, a posh sort of family, Rowing – that was their surname, not what they did for a living. And their youngest was a little gal, named Jolly Knickers or JK for short.

Well... you can imagine... I suggested to JK that she came out onto the rugger pitch with myself, my siblings and Nanny Bob for a bit of practice. And so we all had a bit of a game. Fumbling balls more often than not, as it was a rather muddy sort of afternoon. Then Nanny Bob took the ball and ran with it. On and on she went, he went, making for the touchline and the only person who could stop her, the only person in the way, was Jolly Knickers.

Now, to her credit, JK did make a fine old tackle. And Nanny Bob was brought crashing down.

The trouble was, Nanny Bob's shorts came crashing down too.

That's the sort of thing that can happen in rugby. Part of the fun, even.

Anyway, JK, expecting to see... well... girly bits... had an absolute screaming fit. As you can well imagine. And from that day to this, even though she went on to write the odd paperback and had some limited success at doing so, I don't think she ever got over the shock of seeing a chap dressed as a girl.

And that too, of course, was also the end of Nanny Bob.

And from then on, I had to go to a proper school.

But what a rotten sort of show that place was!

......

......

......

Now a lot of people think of Eton (also the likes of Harrow, Rugby and what have you) as a proper toffee-nosed place, where only super-rich kids go, before they spend a few years dossing around at Oxford or Cambridge, prior to going on to take all the top jobs, all the top salaries and run the country – most of them without the slightest suitable qualification for doing so!

Well, all of that is quite true.

But what a wheeze, eh, for those of us wealthy enough to manage the requisite few terms there?

In my own case, Mater and Pater couldn't wait to see the back of me. And so I was dressed up like a proper count – have I misspelled that word? It doesn't look quite right – and shunted off to full board at Eton.

To be fair, it wasn't just that my parents couldn't stand the sight of me. (Though, often, they couldn't.) The thing you need to realise, with really really really wealthy parents, like mine, is that they have better things to do than bring up their snotty little brats. So we have a Nanny as soon as poss, then we are farmed out to one school after another, where we are kept as far away, for as long as humanly possible, from our parents. That gives the old folk time to go off and exploit a third world nation or become head of an oil giant (which, to be fair, also means exploiting third world nations) or head of an arms manufacturer (ditto), rather than faff about with their kids. All the time, of course. making more millions, for the family.

So that was me. Dressed up like a cartoon character, I was smartly packed off to Eton.

A word or two about Eton: there is a myth that homosexuality is rife at places like Eton. That it is, more or less, compulsory. Coming far ahead of subjects such as French or Mathematics or Physics in the curriculum. The myth goes on to say that is why, once us rich kids leave those expensive schools behind, we often become so hostile towards the LGBTQ community. The myth being that it is quite one thing to spend a few years at school playing the flute, so to speak, for senior boys – but quite another to expect the same sort of practices to be permitted elsewhere in society.

Myths, of course, are just that. Myths. Which is funny old word, when you think about it. A bit like rhythm. Where is the vowel? I have no idea. There must be one hidden in those words somewhere, and my own theory is that the letter 'h' works as the vowel. But tiff tiff, I am digressing.

......

......

......

But no account of my Eton days would be complete, however, without giving you an insight into my character.

Every now and then, the beaks thought it was a grand idea to invite the old folk around, for an hour or two, in order to let them know how badly their kids were getting on.

My parents were no exception. They flew in from Dubai and Hong Kong, on a specially chartered plane, and popped along in a limo to have a word, as it were. A word, and a glass or two of sherry.

What, then, was the general opinion of the masters regarding yours truly? Well, it will surprise all of you to hear that they regarded me as complacent, idle and more or less useless.

I know! I know! Doesn't that just go to prove how wrong school reports can be!

......

......

......

So yes, I gave that nonsense up, and instead I joined the Bullying Club. A latter day version of the 17th Century Hellfire Club. Booze, birds and lots of the aforesaid boister.

I should be frank here. Not any old oick can join the Bullying Club. But nor is it *just* a class based, establishment supporting bunch of toffee nosed tossers. Oh no! Because a fair few of those are not allowed to join the Bullying Club either! You have to pass a range of tests to be allowed in. Being stinking rich and rather offensive is only the very start of your admission process. From that point on, there are various things you must do; a sort of ongoing, gradual initiation, so to speak.

Naturally, I cannot go into the details of that same aforementioned admission process here. Oink, oink. Rather like the Masons, it is all pretty secret stuff. A way of keeping you, the proles, out of power. But I will give you a rough outline... well, a few choice words... teasers almost... and you must just let your imaginations put them together in any way you choose. And, who knows, you may even be right:

*midnight, candles, animal husbandry, large sack of birdseed, wallpaper paste, step-ladder and, lastly, a galvanised bucket*

And with that, and with a large, well-filled brown envelope arriving too late for me to be awarded a First Class degree, I left Oxford, none the bloody wiser.

......

......

......

And it was thus that, one day, whilst sitting at a rather pleasant little pavement cafe, or to be accurate slumped after a heavy lunch and close to chucking it all back up again, that I had a meeting which went on to shape the rest of my life. My life thus far, anyway.

Here is that story in full: the sun was out, the andouillette had not yet gone all the way down and yes, as admitted above, I did feel like emptying the can all over the pavement. Too much ouzo. That sort of thing. And I actually believe that I would have done that but for the timely intervention of the chum of an old chum from some public school or other.

Yakob – his real name was Walter, but ever since some upset during his school days which involved a copy of The Beano and one of the older boys taking the role of a *very* dominant Dennis, he had preferred to be called Yakob – was a beastly little horror. A proper little tit. And that much, I am sure, he would not mind my making quite clear. He is, after all, still a beastly little horror and a proper little tit and he makes no attempt whatsoever to disguise that fact as far as I can see. Anyway, this chap, Yakob Pea-Fogg, was on the verge of tears.

I tried to calm him down, telling him to chin-up, square-jaw, stiff-upper-lip, and all of that rot. But it simply didn't work.

So we bought a carafe of Chateau Lafleur (1951 – I had been forced to quaff the last of the 1950 earlier in an attempt to wash down that blasted sausage) and we had a good old chat.

It turned out that Yakob was hugely worried. About money of all things. A topic about which I had certainly never given a moment's thought.

What was the trouble? Well, apparently, the European Union wanted to clamp down, hugely, on tax evasion... tax avoidance... tax dodging... whatever. Take your pick. It all means the same.

"So what?" I asked.

I really could not see his problem.

All of the richest folk, shovel barrowfulls of lolly overseas and hide it at every available opportunity. And they have been doing that since the arrival of Beloved Maggie in 1979. That, after all, is why the country is running out of money, almost on its uppers, and that is why you ordinary folk have to keep on paying more and more, for less and less.

If the EU, with which at that time I had absolutely no issue, wanted to clampdown on that, a tad, then so what? It might even keep a few village libraries open. Most of the loot would be moved to the Bahamas or wherever anyway and the EU would only get their hands on a bit of the stuff.

But no. Yakob was adamant. There was no way – and he was insistent about that *no way* – that anybody, anywhere, would get their hands on as much as a sou of the Pea-Foggs' fortune. That was what he kept telling me, as the wine went down and the night drew on.

"Not one bloody penny", he said. "Why should we give over any of our hard-earned lolls to that lot?"

I yawned at that point. The whole thing was getting far too political for me, and that sort of stuff bored me rigid. And I did not even try to disguise the fact that I was looking at my watch again.

But that was the very moment at which his rather dreary tale became interesting, because he then said that "many others, like me, like my family, lots of them... influentials... all feel the same...".

Well. My ears pricked up.

"Really?" I said.

"Yes", he replied. And he went on to name some of them.

Well. Again, you can imagine. It transpired that all of those rich and powerful folk were getting together to drag Blighty out of the EU, in order to avoid paying a bit more tax.

"Won't that trash the economy?" I asked.

Yakob shrugged. "It might", he admitted. "But who cares? So long as our loot is safe...".

I nodded. That made sense to me.

"So what is the problem?" I asked.

"We've no leader", he whined. "We are the sort of folk, as well you know, who would pick an argument in an empty phone booth. Horrid, self-serving sorts we are. And so we can't agree on a leader".

And that, right there, right then, was where my own deep-seated, reasoned and thoroughly principled ambition to become Prime Minister was born.

......

......

......

I was Mayor of London for eight years. I think. Or was it longer? It certainly felt like longer!

What did I do during that time?

Oo, I did all sorts. All sorts. Like. Like er... Like erm... well... I was on TV, quite often. And.... er... I had a brilliant idea for a bridge or a tunnel. I forget which it was now. Either way around , I spaffed an absolute fortune in consultation fees for that idea. Whatever it was. And, as far as I can recall, I did much the same on lots of other similarly half-baked ideas too. Consultants loved me.

......

......

......

As Prime Minister, my first job was indeed to do something about Brexit.

I had no real idea what that 'something' would be, or even could be, but by that time it didn't matter. Not a jot. Why not? Because the referendum had been held three whole years earlier, and people just wanted something doing, anything, just get something done, one way or the other, anything, they had voted for a mess (and no, I don't mean me, I mean the EU referendum!) and now they wanted that mess sorting out.

Politically, on the one side, we had Catweazle as head of the Labour party. So he, pretty obviously, was going nowhere. Least of all into Number 10. So it was down to me to resolve the thing.

How best do that? Call a General Election.

So that was what I did.

On paper, that election itself was a straightforward choice between 'Getting Brexit done' (our nonsensical slogan) or 'Prolong the pain of doing nothing' (the oppositions official position). But in reality – as I have already intimated – the election was much more about a straightforward choice: 'Do you want Catweazle for Prime Minister or Boris'?

And the resounding answer from the British public was 'Boris'.

So, I won that General Election, dashed once more through the door to Downing Street before people realised the enormous gaff they had made, and then got Brexit done.

Who was it that said you can't fool all of the people all of the time!

......

......

......

So there we are.

And what of the future?

Well, my replacement, Thick Lizzy, won't last long. That much you can be sure of. And she will soon be followed into office by somebody or other from the Labour party. In opposition, a succession of Tory looneys and losers will come and go. And then, the party – indeed the country! – will surely see sense and come back for me, and I shall return to power. Triumphant. Possibly even carried aloft on a palanquin like a veritable Caesar.

Until that happy day arrives? Well... I dare say I shall make a few bob waffling on at various places, both here and abroad. Spilling the beans on a few juicy bits of gossip.

Giving the odd top CEO a bit of good advice. Who knows? I may even, possibly, be offered the position as head of NATO, or even the UN? Why, I wouldn't be at all surprised if................

# Lights out

At her last birthday, she was 96 years old.

A grand old age. That was what everybody said. Which it was, which it was.

But what did *she* think about that?

"Life is too short in a way. Even if you do reach this age, my age I mean, what they call a grand old age, it is still too short. We... that is, I, spent the first fifth of my life, really, as a youngster, as a child in one form or another. Twenty years. The best part of it. We all do that. Naturally, we don't think we are still a child when we are sixteen or what have you, but we are. Even to that age of twenty. Which is, when you look at it, still a very young age. Just look at the faces of most twenty year olds. They appear so young and fresh.

"Then, from the age of... oh... well, that varies... but from your mid fifties, more or less, onwards, you *are* old. And there is no escaping that fact. In one form or another, you are old. The reverse of being young. We don't feel old at sixty, perhaps, but we are. Yes we are".

Overall, then? Twenty years a child. And once arrived in mid-fifties, old. So that makes, what, only around thirty five years neither young nor old. It isn't much, is it. Not very long at all.

The old lady smiled. Thought about that. Then nodded her head in agreement. "Yes. Exactly. And it always felt to me that God, or whoever, depending on your religion or viewpoint, could have done a slightly better job in that way. For me, I think it would have been much nicer, much kinder, you know, fairer, if we reached maturity at about ten years, and stayed that way, young, strong and fit, until we were about ninety or so. And then, quite quickly, we could slip away into old age. Dwindle down rapidly. Yes. Yes, to me, I often felt that would be better".

Less time young, a shorter time old?

"Oh yes. Definitely. And a much longer time in the middle!"

She laughed. As she had always laughed. Always had to laugh, to be fair, because there were always trials and tribulations in her life. As in every life. But certainly such things were plentiful in a life that ran on for so very many years.

So how did she feel, how did 'it' feel to reach such a fine old age?

"Well I don't feel any different now, not really, to when I was a young girl. Not only is life, or at least that middle part of life, too short, but the years also go by so quickly. They really do. Again, it is impossible to believe that when you are young, but they do. Yes, they really do. I recall that, when I was only in my teens, an aunt or close relative died and — now I know you will laugh at this, but it is a true story — and a friend of mine who was staying with us, at that time, when my aunt or whoever died, said that my auntie had a message for me. From the other side, so to speak. I was sceptical, of course I was, but I listened anyway. And do you know what that message was?"

No. I'm afraid not. Please do tell me.

"Well, apparently my late aunt had taken a moment to return from the other side, the other place, wherever it is we go when we die, to inform me; 'Be sure to live your life to the full, because it goes by, passes by, so very very quickly. And you — by which she meant me — are now only a young girl, and it all seems to stretch out, ahead of you. And that is true. It does. Life does lie, mostly, ahead of you. But that time will fly by. It will simply fly by'".

And was she right? Did your years fly by?

"Oh yes", said the grand old lady. "Absolutely. And that is one thing I would love to get across to everyone, especially to the young folk. I understand their stresses, their rebelliousness. It is good and it is healthy. But they should never lose sight of the fact that time really does go by so very quickly. Life goes by. You won't even notice it, until it has gone. Not unless you keep yourself aware and enjoy every single moment... well... not necessarily enjoy, but certainly savour. Savour it all. For it is too soon gone".

Your husband died, only last year, I believe?

"Yes".

He was a good age, too, wasn't he?

"Yes, indeed. A very good age. Even older than I am now! He was an incredible 99 years old when he died".

Wow! Ninety-nine.

"Yes. I know. Isn't that something?"

How many years were the two of you married? And do you miss him? I guess you must do.

"We married way, way back in 1947. And so, all told, we were together for 74 years, in total. We often felt that it must be some sort of a record. But no, it wasn't. Far from it. There are lots of other people who have been married that long and, some, even longer.

"But you asked me if I miss him? Yes. I do. Of course I do. But then, in a strange way, I rather feel as if he is still here, you know, still with me. And I also feel sure, well, as sure as one can, that we will be together again in the not so distant future".

I nodded agreement to that. Not my place to say if it was true, one way or the other. But it felt right. In any case, why not believe as much? It was a good, wholesome and healthy belief. And not one person, ever, would be able to prove it right or wrong. So why believe the worst of things? I smiled. And I replied quite simply; 'Yes, yes, I am sure you are right'.

"The thing I do miss though... ," the grand old lady continued, and quite without my prompting, "are those moments, you know, where two people, as any couple will tell you, as any close couple will tell you, can almost step aside from the rush and noise of the world, and share a moment or two with each other. Let the troubles of life fall away for a few precious seconds or minutes of peace. That, yes, I do miss".

I understood. But then I wondered about family. So I asked her. You have your family, though? Friends too?

"Yes, yes, I do. Yes, that's true. Though they never, with the best will in the world, quite take the place of your partner, least of all, as I say, if you are close as a couple. And if you have spent so many years together, as we had done".

Time was passing.

But I wanted to ask a few more questions.

So I allowed myself the opportunity to do so.

And what would you change, if anything, about your life?

The old lady considered that question for a moment or two. I waited patiently for her to do so.

"Well...", she finally began, "I am sure there are very many things, in every life, that could be done better. We, all of us, far too often, only think of ourselves in a given situation, a given moment or event. And we act accordingly, don't we? It would be good if we could, somehow, revisit those events a little later, and say and do the things we wished we had said and done instead. Not always, no, but often enough for that to be a bit of a regret. For me. Indeed for everyone, I should imagine."

Ah, really? And do you have an example of such?

She considered her reply for a moment or two. "No, no. Nothing I can or would be prepared to point to. Not really. I will admit that I could have done more. At times. Let's just leave it at that".

Do you wish you had been born otherwise?

At that, the old woman's face, briefly, lit up. A smile.

I smiled too.

"Do you mean, born into a normal little home, to do a normal job, full of insecurity, with scant thanks and even less recognition? No. No I would not wish to have lived such a life".

Yet most do live such lives. Almost all, in fact.

"Yes, I know. And I will be frank with you. I do feel, in all truthfulness, that anybody could have done what I did.

Despite what they all say. Well... almost anybody. But you do need to be born into this family, into this whole situation. Because it begins from day one, almost, and it would be hard, if not impossible... yes... I think impossible, to be parachuted into this role. You need to be born to it".

Are all men equal?

"And women?"

Of course.

"Yes".

But your life was not one of equality. You had all one could wish for, whilst so many others have nothing. Did that never trouble you?

"No. Not really, no. I wish that others had plenty, I wish that nobody suffered, that nobody went without. Of course I wish all that, yes. But I was never troubled, in that way, by my own position in this life. Because, at the end of the day, as your presence here confirms, it is only *this life*, isn't it?"

I nodded my head. Agreed.

And that, really, was enough for now.

The day was coming to its close. And I had very many other calls to make. So I rose to leave the room.

I paused for a moment to look out of the window, across the autumnal lawns and, beyond them, into the dark forests which surrounded this fine old house.

It would soon be winter, I thought. Winter. And yes, the old lady was right about time. Time flies by. It really does. And the seasons reflect that urgency. If only time would slow down a little... for all of us. But no, perhaps not, for that would be like asking the sun to change colour or the rain to fall upwards. We cannot have the world we want, we must all adapt to the world we have.

I turned to look at the old lady. Ninety-six years old. She was a grand old lady, alright. That much was true. But more than that? Who she was, the money she had, the power, whatever, it did not matter one jot to me. Not one jot. I had known worse than her — but I had also known better.

I yawned.

And with that, she yawned too. A small, but polite yawn.

And then I told her — flatly, because there is no other way to do it and that was how I always did it — that her time was up too. Right there. Right then. I could not wait around, chatting, any longer. There were other people who I had to see. Their times were up too. And one of them was only a young girl. Young like this lady once had been.

Well, the old lady smiled at my news.

She nodded her head.

She understood that her time was done.

Yes, she did.

And with that, she closed her eyes and died.

And with that, I walked out of that elegant room. Turning the lights out as I left.

# Primeval stewage

This story begins on a chilly Friday evening, in late September.

For some years prior to the evening in question, water companies had been having rather a laugh at the expense of their customers. Charging more, ever more, for an ever worse service.

There was nothing new in that. Not really. The same skulduggery had been going on with electric, gas and things like rail ever since such essential services had been farmed out to private concerns.

However, whereas late, grubby and expensive trains were depressing, and whereas unaffordable electric and gas led to Good Old Victorian things like fuel poverty and frostbite, water, really, was quite something else and all those years of neglect and regulation dodging had led to a number of ill effects.

The first ill effect? Water quality had gone down and...

The second ill effect? Water leaks had gone up.

Now these two things did have one thing in common. Of course they did. For instance, leaks were no longer repaired, because that took a few pennies away from the profits for shareholders. Likewise, new systems to provide better water and so forth were not invested in for much the same reason.

But there was a third, hidden, grimmer, grimier, and altogether more sinister 'ill effect' of water privatisation and the concomitant neglect of that service: namely sewage.

It is quite one thing to provide water, clean or cleanish, via a tap or toilet. Everybody can see whether or not they have water. Turn on your tap, right now, and find out for yourself.

But waste? That's an altogether different matter. We flush the loo, drain the kitchen sink, washing machine, dishwasher, whatever, and then we think no more about it. Waste disappears from our surface world, to enter a dark subterranean land of tunnels and rats and fatbergs and goodness knows what else besides. And down there, we think, we hope, is where it somehow stays. Being managed, more or less, by those same people who provide our running water in a rather haphazard manner.

Only it isn't being managed. Not really. Not any more. Because those same aforementioned private companies quickly realised that 'out of sight, is out of mind'. And it was all too easy for them to simply pump nasty things like sewage out into a river, or into the sea rather than do anything constructive with the stuff.

Now, that was one thing. Polluting rivers and beaches.

But what of those dark drains and sewers themselves? The drains under our streets, under our homes, under your home where you may be sitting right now and reading this story.

Forgotten. Ignored. Not invested in.

So what about all that fat, that waste, the poop, the chemicals, the gases? Nastiness in all shapes and sizes. A veritable soup of organic matter, down there, in those drains, simmering away at a constant temperature, just waiting for that spark which gives it life. Melding slowly together. Becoming something... something else... something greasy, smelly, sinister and perhaps, one day, even alive.

But I am getting ahead of myself...


Friday evening. 23rd September. 2022.

Mr and Mrs Tippins were sitting down to watch their usual TV favourites. Over a hearty post-Brexit meal of dry bread and stale cheese, they sipped a single glass of water and waited for the soaps to start.

But first, of course, the news came on. A quick catch-up on the days events and the nonsensical mini-budget.

*'Huge amount of money given to very richest'.* Well, that was the headline.

This news, as ever, the Tippins' largely chose to ignore.

Mr Tippins did tut and shake his head. And he did wonder, for a while, whether *he* was one of the aforementioned 'richest'. After all, he had worked all his life, paid into a pension, owned his own bungalow and even voted Conservative. So, and furtively, as his wife turned off a light or two elsewhere in the house to save some electric, he checked the 'Who benefits most' calculator.

Needless to say, he did *not* benefit most.

Not even second most. Third most. Tenth most. Anywhere most.

"Good news?" said Mrs Tippins as she returned to her threadbare chair, to wait for her own sip of the water. "About the budget, I mean?"

"Bah! It would have been. But its all Labours fault", said Mr Tippins. "When they were last in office, blah blah blah and blah...".

Mrs Tippins smiled. She avoided politics like the plague. Besides, she had heard it all before. "When was that?" she asked, in all innocence. "That they were last in office, I mean".

Mr Tippins couldn't remember. Not really. And it was, in truth, a very long time ago. "Bah! You wont see me voting for the Socialists", he said.

The news then finished. And after some other bits and bobs, the soaps finally started. And the two pensioners settled down to watch, shivering a little as they did so, with it being late September and the heating being quite definitely, unaffordably off.

And that was the moment at which a foul, malodorous and totally pungent stench suddenly and quite abruptly filled their not-so-cosy little living room

"Goodness me", said Mr Tippins. "I think that dry bread must have disagreed with you, dear".

"Oh no, dear", said Mrs Tippins, "That isn't me. I'm afraid that must be you".

"No. It was *not* me", said Mr Tippins, rather angrily. "And I told you the cheese would do that. Your digestion is not what it was, Mrs T".

The smell itself was indeed quite ghastly. Of that there could be no question. It was definite, distinct, it was eggy, and it was sulphurous. It was as unmissable as a sausage in a hot dog or as a dog poop in a snow drift. And in a way, as there were only two of them in the house, it was quite natural that Mr Tippins had assumed that it was his wife, whilst she had assumed that it was her husband.

In truth, however, it was neither of them as a sudden crashing sound from their kitchen appeared to confirm.

"Burglars!" said Mrs Tippins, her voice all a tremor. "We've got burglars".

Was it burglars? Was it truly the case that one or more people had entered the Tippins home and, in the midst of their thievery, had somehow created an obnoxious odour?

That thought, like the stench, hung in the air.

The thought, however, quickly dissipated. Unlike the stench.

"No. It can't be burglars", said Mr Tippins, finally. "They're hardly going to stand around in the kitchen passing wind, are they? Go in and see what it is. Its probably that cat from next door. You'll have put some milk down for it again, no doubt, and then left the kitchen window open for it".

Mrs Tippins, knowing that she had done exactly that, felt somewhat reassured by her husbands words.

She got up, slowly, and made her way into the kitchen.

And that was the last anyone ever saw of her.


"And when did you realise that she had... well... disappeared?" said the Police Sergeant, seated where Mrs Tippins usually sat.

"She went into the kitchen", said Mr Tippins. "The soaps started. I watched them. The first one finished. I wondered where she was. I had assumed she had gone to the lav. You know. That strange smell I mentioned".

The Sergeant nodded his head.

"But when I went to see.... she wasn't there. She was nowhere."

"Popped out?" said the Sergeant.

Mr Tippins shook his head. "We never go out after dark. We close the curtains, get the big light on, get settled. It isn't safe outside for us old folk outside, you know. Says so, in the papers".

"So... she just vanished, then?" said the Sergeant.

"Yes", said Mr Tippins.

To the Sergeant, and the constable with him, it all seemed highly unlikely.

People did not simply disappear.

Leastways, not indoors.

"Do you have a cellar?" asked the constable. "A garage?"

"No", said Mr Tippins. "Neither thing".

"She went into the kitchen?"

"Yes. I told you. To see what made the noise".

"Shall we go and see?"

The three of them stood, and walked into the kitchen.

Into what was a perfectly ordinary, small, slightly dated, kitchen of the sort found in most homes, the length and breadth of the country.

The Sergeant walked over to the window. It was firmly shut. Locked even.

"I closed that", said Mr Tippins.

Then the Sergeant tried the back door. Same story.

"We never dare unlock that, after dark".

The three of them went out into the back garden, anyway. Which was tiny.

But clearly, Mrs Tippins was not out there, either.

Back in the kitchen, there was nothing unusual to be seen. Nothing. Nothing unusual except for a trail of oil or grease on the floor, which led from the middle of the room, to the kitchen sink. A broad trail. Thickish. Rather like those trails which snails and slugs leave behind.

"You should clean that up", said the Sergeant. "Someone could slip on it".

Mr Tippins looked down at the trail of fat. "I don't know what that is", he said. "We haven't had any oil, or fat, or lard or anything for weeks. Cant afford it. You know how it is, these days. We only ever have dry bread".

"I'll clean it up", said the Constable. "Save your old back".

And so that was what he did.


Some days passed. And no sign was found of Mrs Tippins.

The Police searched.

They put up missing person notices.

They checked the whole house again, from top to bottom.

But there was nothing. Nothing at all.

And then one evening, in early October, old Mr Tippins was sitting watching TV again. This time he was all alone, and had even pushed the boat out and made himself a piece of toast to go with his water, when that same smell, that same ghastly smell suddenly re-appeared in his little home.

"Ugh", he said, reluctantly pushing his meagre supper to one side. "What on earth is that pong? I think Mrs Tippins must have been right all along. It must be me."

On this occasion, Mr Tippins fully intended to ignore the smell. After all, he was in his own home, alone, and if a man cannot quietly stink out his own house, then it's a poor state of affairs, isn't it?

Besides, the soaps were about to start. And he was settled.

But then the smell got worse.

And worse.

Until it was, frankly, eggily, wholly unbearable.

"Bah! That isn't me", said Mr Tippins, grumpily, and getting out of his chair, heading for the kitchen. "Must be something wrong with the drains".

At that very moment came the most awful, horrendous waowling sound. Brief, yes, but quite horrible.

"Goodness me", said Mr Tippins, rushing into the kitchen, from whence the sound, not to mention the smell, appeared to be coming.

But in the kitchen there was nothing to be seen.

Nothing.

The window was open. Mr Tippins had accidentally left it open after burning his toast, so unused was he to having such luxury foodstuff in modern-day Britain.

There was a trail of fat or grease or something leading from the kitchen sink across the floor and even, in one place, some way up the wall.

But other than that? There was nothing.

"At least that smell seems to have gone", said Mr Tippins to himself, as he closed the window. "Must have been that bloody cat. Been catching mice or something, I bet. Its my own fault, for leaving that blasted window open".

He turned away from the window, took the very last (cheap) biscuit from a scruffy little tin, and headed back to the living room and the TV.

He hadn't reached either thing, however, before there was a knock at the front door.

"Who the devil is that? At this hour".

Cursing under his breath, a little, Mr Tippins opened the thing.

"Hello Mr Tippins", said Mrs Finch, the old lady who lived next door. "I'm sorry to trouble you, but George... this is going to sound very odd... George has disappeared".

"George?" said Mr Tippins, momentarily confused. "Oh, your husband you mean. George".

"Yes", said Mrs Finch. "He's not here, is he? We were sitting watch TV. He got up to go to the kitchen... there was such an awful smell coming from in there... and... but somehow, he didn't come back. And he's not in the house. Nor even the shed or the garden. I wondered, perhaps he had popped around here. But then... that business with your wife...".

Mr Tippins shook his head. He was missing the soaps.

"No", he said flatly. "He isn't here".

"It's all very odd", said Mrs Finch. "You must know the Harrison's across the road? The night before last, or so it appears, Mr Harrison went upstairs to the loo and he, too, has never been seen since".

Mr Tippins frowned. He had never liked the Harrisons. Socialists, he called them.

"Probably down the pub", he muttered, grouchily.

Mrs Finch nodded. "Yes. Perhaps that is it".

Mr Tippins not-too-gently ushered Mrs Finch a few steps back towards the open front door.

"Oh, and Tiddles has gone too", said Mrs Finch. "I don't suppose you've seen her?"

Mr Tippins shrugged. Tiddles was the cat who, far too often for Mr Tippins liking came into *his* kitchen. "Like I said, try the bloody pub", and with that, he closed the front door and went back to his place in front of the TV.

"Dratted woman", he muttered as he picked up the remote control.

The interminable adverts were on. Evidently, he had missed the first part of the first of the evening soaps.

"I suppose I might as well nip to the loo myself", he said.

And as he slowly climbed the stairs, the night sky darkening outside, a hiss of cars in the street, a damp evening, he singularly failed to notice the obvious, obnoxious, drainy sort of stench which was now emanating, with a sordid sort of gurgling sound, from the direction of his bathroom. The same room which also housed the toilet...

# No such thing...

Once upon a time, there was a gardener.

Well, OK, maybe that isn't quite accurate. But there was an old man, actually a middle-aged man, who had lost his job and was struggling to find another. He was struggling to find another because he had no great skills, nothing that was particularly marketable, no CV, no driving licence, no car and he was a socially shy sort of person.

None of that should have made him worthless, however. Because, really, when you think about it, it is up to Society to create roles for such people, rather than throw them on the scrapheap, for otherwise what is the point of society? If it is only there for folk who are already doing well, then it has lost it's purpose... But I am digressing. This isn't an ideal world, far from it, and so the man was, in the employment sense of things, quite quite worthless.

Or so it seemed.

In fairness to this particular middle-aged man, however, being of no obvious use didn't matter all that much to him. He was more or less used to being a failure in such ways. He knew that society didn't really want him, didn't really need him, because it never had. And he was quite accepting of that. In truth, there are very many millions of folk who society feels that way about. And this particular middle-aged man was just another one of those.

To this man, unemployed or not, life would go on as it always had. He would be short of money, short of luxuries, not take a holiday, and he would go without most of the things he had always gone without, whether in work or not. Sooner or later, he was sure of it, some little job would come up. And then life would resume it's usual impoverished shape.

Fortitude. That was what he had. Fortitude. Because even in such seemingly unimportant people, great traits can always be found.

Anyway. Time slowly passed. And the man remained unemployed.

Now although certain newspapers, certain media outlets, certain political parties and certain ideologies will tell you that 'not having a job' means you are idle... that does not necessarily follow. Sometimes, yes, it is true. Some folk who don't have a job *are* idle. But then, so are plenty of folk who do have jobs. And the truth is that very many people who are, technically, unemployed, actually fill their time in the most constructive of ways.

They work for voluntary organisations.

They look after their aged parents.

They babysit for friends.

They busy themselves with innumerable pastimes, such as stamp collecting, model making, cooking, watching TV, reading, writing or even gardening.

(All, pretty much, harmless occupations. If only the same could be said about very many paid positions! After all, there is nothing whatsoever harmless about manufacturing weapons or pesticides or issuing exploitative loans to third world countries. And yet the people who do such horrible jobs are not criticised for being 'idle'. Would that they were so! The world would be a better place. But once again I am digressing...).

And just like those others, so too had this particular middle-aged man also gotten himself a harmless and, if anything, rather useful little hobby; realising that he would be out of work for some time, and not wanting to spend his days indoors, neither learning a new skill nor getting any fresh air and exercise, he had gone to the local town council and applied for an allotment. A small plot of land, upon which men — because it is usually men — grow a variety of fruit and vegetables.

Now this man knew nothing at all about growing plants. So the next trip he made was to the local library. Where he took out a couple of books about how to grow vegetables.

He studied those books carefully. Made notes.

And then he spent some of his very limited budget on various packets of seeds and a few second hand (but still good) garden tools.

As it was winter — and not a time to sow seeds — he then spent a hard few hours, digging over the plot of land which the council had given him. Preparing the soil, as all good gardeners must, for the coming season.

And sure enough, by the following spring, with that soil on his allotment well and truly prepared, he was ready to start growing his own vegetables.

Now, what you sow on an allotment, or even in your garden, depends upon both your local climate and also on the sort of soil you have. If you want your plants to thrive you need plenty of sun, but also lots of moisture, and you also need a good soil which, ideally, is neither too heavy nor too thin.

Of course there isn't a lot you can do about soil or climate, though both can be helped a little with some shade or a good watering can, or with the addition of manure and so on.

And so this man did what he could.

He had already manured the soil back in the winter. He had then worked the stuff down into a fine old tilth. He had bought a watering can and his friend had given him a hosepipe. So, really, he was all set and ready to go.

Then, and following a rough but pretty accurate timetable, he began to sow his seeds.

But there was one other thing which he wanted to try; something that other gardeners, some other gardeners, believed to be nonsense, whilst yet others swore by it. What was it? He would talk to his seeds as he planted them and then, when they appeared above ground, he would talk to the little plants. And, as they grew bigger, he would talk to them even more. All the time telling them — the lettuces, the cabbages and carrots, the peas and the beans — just whatever positive thoughts came into his head.

He would tell them that the sun would feel nice, if they grew big and strong.

He would tell them that the rain would feel lovely, especially after a few dry days.

He would promise them 'feed' if they seemed to need it.

And he told them what weeds were, as he removed suchlike from the allotment.

In short, the middle-aged man, though not a natural gardener, did his very best to make his plants thrive.

And thrive they did!


"He really is very good to us", said the biggest of the lettuces, one afternoon, as the gardener came into sight, parking his old pushbike by a rickety little shed, which had been left on the allotment by a previous owner. "He was here all afternoon, yesterday. And now, look, he is back again today. Bringing slug pellets, I'll be bound. And just when I need them too".

Slugs, in recent days, had started to devour the young shoots of some other plants, before spotting the two tidy rows of lettuces and making their greedy way across to them.

The gardener tried to look after his small plot of land, the best way he could, without using chemicals. But slugs? No. That was the one exception. They wreaked havoc, according to all the gardening books, and although a thing called a 'beer trap' would catch a few, it would also catch things like bees and wasps, who were generally good friends to the gardener.

So yes, slug pellets it was. It was the only way to deal with that particular pest.

"Here I am", said the gardener, talking to his vegetables, as he always had, "I promised I would come back today, with these. They should make a big difference".

The whole two rows of lettuces leaned, slightly, this way and that, to see what exactly the gardener would do.

And then they watched, in lettucey-awe, as he deftly sprinkled the tiny blue pellets here and there, in amongst them.

"He can do anything", said the biggest lettuce. "That will stop the slugs, you mark my word!"

Next up it was time to give the carrots a good watering.

Yesterday, the gardener had spent hours weeding the plot, and he had more or less run out of time for watering. He had managed a bit, on the lettuces, on the spring onions, and on the radish, but today, he would do a lot more. Because plants like beetroot and carrots need a good bit of water, to get them started. Or else they end up very small and rather woody.

So he got out the hosepipe. And gave the different vegetables a right good soaking.

"Look at that!" said one of the bigger carrots. "He gives us water. Without it we would all die, did you know that? But he goes even further than that, for he gives us so much water that we can grow bigger and stronger. What a being the gardener is! He gave us all life, he sustains us, and...".

At that moment, a great cold shower of water hit the carrots, and stopped them from chattering.

But they didn't mind. Not at all. They loved it!

It was life giving water. And lots of it.

"I can't spend all day here, today", said the gardener, a little while later, after the watering was done, "As I have been summoned to the Job Centre, I think they have a job offer for me. Which is no bad thing, as I could use the extra money".

The rows of vegetables had no idea what money was.

Nor did they know, nor care, what a Job Centre was.

And they watched, they all watched, in awe, once more, as the gardener then busied himself placing a half dozen bamboo posts in the ground, for the runner beans to grow up.

"Oh my!" said a small, fat onion, "Just look at that! He is shaping our very world for us, for the beans this time, so they can grow better. He is building towers, almost, of bamboo. Without such, they would surely trail along the ground and not flourish".

"He thinks of everything", said another onion. "He can *do* everything! No matter what the need, the gardener attends to it. How lucky we all are to have him! Whatever the problem, he is here for us and always has been!"

And all of the vegetables agreed with that.

Even the smallest of the peas nodded it's little green head. "Yes", it said. "He obviously loves us".

And that, in a way, was true.

Of course it was.

The gardener cared about all of his vegetables.

He wanted them all to thrive.

Of course he did.

But life is never quite as straightforward as we — or even as carrots, leeks and cabbage — would like it to be.

And the gardener had to report to the Job Centre later on that very afternoon to pick up the details for a job interview. And, as he was a conscientious sort of chap, and not keen on having his meagre benefits stopped, that was exactly what he did.

He finished his work, for the day, on the allotment and went straight from there to the Job Centre.

Once there he picked up the details of the job interview which, to his dismay, involved travelling almost two hours to a small company who manufactured cheap, unhealthy and sugary biscuits.

"Oh dear", he said to himself as he cycled home. "This interview is tomorrow. First thing. I'd be more than glad of the work, but I do wish that the job was not so far away. And it only pays the minimum wage too. Oh dear. That will mean twelve hours a day, including my travel, plus a lunch hour, five days a week... for very little money. And, worse than that, I shall be mightily worn out from such a long working week. Oh dear me".

But there was something else troubling the gardener too. For not only was the job one of those dead-end sort of affairs, packing biscuits, for that is what it entailed, but it would also leave very little time for attending to his thriving allotment. And, as if all of that was not bad enough, he had just spotted the first signs of verticillium wilt on his peas. A very destructive fungal disease that could, if left unchecked, quickly wreak havoc on all kinds of vegetables.

"I must do something about that... that wilt... this very weekend", he said to himself as he sat and ate his supper that evening.

The following morning, as early if not earlier than the lark, the gardener caught a bus to the train station, a train to another town, and then another bus to a small red-brick factory on a remote, rural industrial estate.

Two hours all told.

A long old haul.

Needless to say, however, he did get the job.

Not even needing to undergo an interview.

"We always have vacancies", said the manager of the company, a grumpy, red-faced sort, who drove a very large car. "People don't want to work today. That's what it is".

The gardener did not reply, but simply smiled. He had often though that the real problem was not work-shyness, nor was it even wages, but rather that, with house-prices being so extraordinarily high, people could not make ends meet on low wages. Thus there was no incentive to stick around in such jobs, no incentive really to work hard. Lots of folk did work very hard, but they still had to rent a little flat, rather than buy a house with a garden in a nice part of town. And no government seemed to care. Neither Labour, nor Conservative, nor even Liberals. They were all as bad as the other in this respect.

"Here we are", said the grumpy manager, "You, basically, just have to take the packets of biscuits from here, this big pile, and fill up one of these cardboard boxes with them".

For eight hours a day.

Five days a week.

For the bare minimum wage.

Oh dear.

Now the trouble was that the gardener took the job — in part as he had no choice and in part as he was a hard-working man — took it, and worked. And worked. Commuted. And worked. And commuted. And worked. And commuted and worked.

And so the week went on. Until, and given that he was, after all, already middle-aged, he felt absolutely worn out.

Totally shattered.

And when the weekend came around, all he could do was sleep.

"I must go and see about my fruit and veg", he said to himself, turning over in bed, late on Sunday afternoon.

But he didn't do that.

Instead he simply fell asleep again.

And by the time he awoke, it was Monday morning. And that meant another week of working, commuting, working, commuting, working, commuting and working. And another week of feeling utterly and completely exhausted. Unable, on any evening, to even visit his allotment.

"I will go this weekend", he said to himself. "I must go and water my plants. It has been so dry lately. And I must get something to treat that fungal disease".

Then he sneezed.

Coughed a few times.

And the following day, he came down with a nasty bout of cold. Bad enough, needless to say, to keep the poor fellow in bed for a few days. Two of which were the very next weekend.

So, once more, the allotment went without his special care and attention.


Now this went on for a couple of weeks. And those weeks became almost a whole month.

The gardener, who now packed cheap biscuits for a poor living, was always elsewhere, either working, commuting, sleeping or feeling unwell.

And of course the allotment began to suffer.

Badly.

"The gardener has forgotten us", said the largest cabbage quietly. It's voice a mix of shock and sadness. "The peas are all dead of wilt".

"All of them?" said the senior carrot. It's voice too, rather subdued and sad.

The cabbage shook one of it's leaves a little, the vegetable equivalent of nodding its head. "Yes. That disease killed them all".

"But... but... but how is that possible?" said the carrot. "Where is the gardener?"

The cabbage had no answer to that.

The rest of the carrots asked one another the same question.

But none of them had an answer.

"Have you seen the lettuces?" said a rather small beetroot. "They are all looking rather shrivelled up. They need water. There has been no rain this week and the gardener has forgotten to come and use that hosepipe thing".

Various vegetables strained to peer and see the rows of lettuce. And yes, sadly, it was true. They were shrivelling up. Quite badly.

"The gardener has forgotten us", said a very puny looking spring onion.

"And there is some of that same fungal disease on the strawberry plants", said another carrot, who was only very, very small.

"No?" said the senior carrot. "Is there? How bad is it?"

The small carrot asked a neighbouring broad bean. And the answer which came back was depressing. "All of them have it. The strawberries are all going to die".

And so it was, one after another, that the different vegetables on the allotment began to realise that they were all, all of them, beginning to struggle and suffer.

The runner beans, for instance, had never been tied to their bamboo poles, and now they lay, all across the ground, rotting and getting tangled, with their beans being eaten by slugs. (The little blue slug pellets long since having been used up).

"If the gardener is, or was, as wonderful, as great, as caring as we all said he was, then why has he allowed this to happen?" said a tall but very, very straggly broccoli plant.

"I thought he could do anything", said another.

"I believed he could do everything", said a third.

But no. Clearly not. The middle-aged man had, for a while, been wholly focussed on the allotment, given it his full attention, but then something else — a horrid little job, packing biscuits — had taken that same focus and attention elsewhere.

He had given all of these plants their life.

He had, in effect, created their entire world.

He had cared for all of them.

But now?

Where was he?

"Why would he leave us to suffer like this?"

"Maybe he is dead", said a very dour looking, and far too undernourished cabbage. "Perhaps the gardener is dead".

"Perhaps there never was a gardener," said the largest cabbage.

And those words, and those sentiments, spread rapidly around the allotment.

And all of the infinite, omnipotent, all-seeing attributes which the vegetables themselves had applied to the gardener, now seemed — in view of the verticillium wilt, drought, slugs and other things — to be little more than nonsensical day-dreaming.

"The gardener doesn't exist!" shouted one.

"There never was a gardener!" cried another.


Another week passed before the gardener, having finally accustomed a little to the horrid long hours and the job, and even then only by virtue of a Bank Holiday, finally managed to find the time and stamina to cycle up to his allotment and get back to work there.

And what a sad, sorry, sad old sight it was.

Enough to bring tears — and it did bring tears — even to the eyes of a world-weary man like the gardener.

Everything was in a tangle. Everything.

And lots of stuff was either dying or dead.

The peas, the lettuce, most of the runner beans... all gone.

Things like beetroot, carrots... all shrunken, woody and nibbled away by slugs.

Cabbage, sprouts... tiny, due to the lack of water.

But worse than that, worse than any of that, worse by far, was that once the gardener set to work, trying to salvage what he could, to try to put right some of the damage and think positively about the future, he found that he was no longer able to talk to the plants.

And, worse still, he had the definite feeling that even if he spoke, they would no longer be able to hear his words.

Thankyou for buying this book!

LOTS more books by the same author (including **Roald Dahl 2021**) are available NOW on Amazon.

"Terribly good and horribly pertinent", Stephen Fry

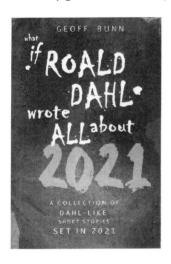

**www.geoffbunn.com**

Printed in Great Britain
by Amazon

12638179R00093